Dani

"So a spouse is included in your future plans?" Reo asked her

"Of course." Rust[...]n yours?"

"Actually, no."

"Are you serious?"

"I don't have time for that kind of commitment. I've got a business to run."

"Oh." She appeared stunned. "But don't you want children?"

"Can't say that I do."

Rusty stared at him as though he were some kind of alien. "I love kids myself. I'm going to marry a wonderful man and have at least four."

"Four!" Reo nearly choked. "You're talking years of childbearing, Rusty. I assume you've already scheduled your Mr. Right for an imminent walk down the aisle. Otherwise you are going to run out of time."

"Thanks for the reality check," Rusty said snappishly, indicating that there was no Mr. Right in sight. But her attitude made one thing clear: she would be a challenge to any man.

And Reo liked challenges....

Dear Reader,

Silhouette Romance is celebrating the month of valentines with six very special love stories—and three brand-new miniseries you don't want to miss. *On Baby Patrol,* our BUNDLE OF JOY selection, by bestselling author Sharon De Vita, is book one of her wonderful series, LULLABIES AND LOVE, about a legendary cradle that brings love to three brothers who are officers of the law.

In *Granted: Big Sky Groom,* Carol Grace begins her sparkling new series, BEST-KEPT WISHES, in which three high school friends' prom-night wishes are finally about to be granted. Author Julianna Morris tells the delightful story of a handsome doctor whose life is turned topsy-turvy when he becomes the guardian of his orphaned niece in *Dr. Dad.* And in Cathleen Galitz's spirited tale, *100% Pure Cowboy,* a woman returns home from a mother-daughter bonding trip with the husband of her dreams.

Next is *Corporate Groom,* which starts Linda Varner's terrific new miniseries, THREE WEDDINGS AND A FAMILY, about long-lost relatives who find a family. And finally, in *With This Child...,* Sally Carleen tells the compelling story of a woman whose baby was switched at birth—and the single father who will do anything to keep his child.

I hope you enjoy all six of Silhouette Romance's love stories this month. And next month, in March, be sure to look for *The Princess Bride* by bestselling author Diana Palmer, which launches Silhouette Romance's new monthly promotional miniseries, VIRGIN BRIDES.

Regards,

Joan Marlow Golan
Senior Editor

Please address questions and book requests to:
Silhouette Reader Service
U.S.: 3010 Walden Ave., P.O. Box 1325, Buffalo, NY 14269
Canadian: P.O. Box 609, Fort Erie, Ont. L2A 5X3

CORPORATE GROOM

Linda Varner

Silhouette

R O M A N C E™

Published by Silhouette Books

America's Publisher of Contemporary Romance

This book is dedicated to Jean Price,
the best of agents and a treasured friend.

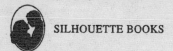 SILHOUETTE BOOKS

ISBN 0-373-19280-0

CORPORATE GROOM

Copyright © 1998 by Linda Varner Palmer

This edition published by arrangement with Harlequin Books S.A.

® and TM are trademarks of Harlequin Books S.A., used under license.
Trademarks indicated with ® are registered in the United States Patent
and Trademark Office, the Canadian Trade Marks Office and in other
countries.

Printed in U.S.A.

Books by Linda Varner

Silhouette Romance

Heart of the Matter #625
Heart Rustler #644
The Luck of the Irish #665
Honeymoon Hideaway #698
Better To Have Loved #734
A House Becomes a Home #780
Mistletoe and Miracles #835
As Sweet as Candy #851
Diamonds Are Forever #868
A Good Catch #906
Something Borrowed #943
Firelight and Forever #966
*Dad on the Job #1036
*Believing in Miracles #1051
*Wife Most Unlikely #1068
†Won't You Be My Husband? #1088
†Mistletoe Bride #1193
†New Year's Wife #1200
‡Corporate Groom #1280

*Mr. Right, Inc.
†Home for the Holidays
‡Three Weddings and a Family

LINDA VARNER

confesses she is a hopeless romantic. Nothing is more thrilling, she believes, than the battle of wits between a man and a woman who are meant for each other but just don't know it yet! Linda enjoys writing romance fiction and considers herself very lucky to have been both a RITA finalist and a third-place winner in the National Readers' Choice Awards in 1993.

A full-time federal employee, Linda lives in Arkansas with her husband and their two children. She loves to hear from readers. Write to her at 813 Oak St., Suite 10A-277, Conway, AR 72032.

SAMPSON FAMILY TREE

Randolf Sampson m. Evelyn Carson

Linette Ashe-------------Jon Sampson m. Sarah Patrick
(a very secret affair)

??   Reo Sampson

From the desk of
Edward Logan Stiles
Attorney-at-Law

Reo—

Spoke to the private investigator today and have more information on your father's alleged affair. If we can track down Ms. Linette Ashe, we might be able to learn if she bore any other children. You do realize that any children of Ms. Ashe's could very well be siblings of yours.

Let's meet to discuss this situation in greater detail, as finding additional family members might have more than just legal ramifications for a wealthy bachelor like yourself.

Edward Logan Stiles

Chapter One

"Hold that elevator!"

Reo Sampson registered with shock the gossamer attire of the red-haired woman scurrying around the corner, calling out to him. He quickly stuffed into his pocket the ID badge he'd just found on the parking deck of his building, then threw out a hand and caught the doors that had been about to close.

So what if he was running a bit late today? No man could resist an elevator ride with an angel—assuming, of course, that's what this woman was supposed to be. The white ankle-length gown that swirled about her with every movement could just as easily costume a fairy, now that he thought about it.

The angel-fairy rewarded Reo's quick action with a smile of thanks so dazzling he wished for his sunglasses. He noted that the color of her long, curly hair exactly matched the coat of an Irish setter who'd once owned him, and for one brief second he was a lonely ten-year-old again with only a dog for a best friend.

"Thanks...a...million," she said, panting even as she stopped and turned her back on him, beckoning to someone still out of sight. "Hurry, kids. Quick as bunnies."

Kids? Reo watched in horror as two...four...six...oh, God, *ten* preschoolers dressed for Mardi Gras immediately filed around the corner and into view. The woman, who looked to be in her late twenties or early thirties, herded them into the elevator, while Reo instinctively flattened himself against one wall of the too-tiny enclosure.

Suddenly they were everywhere, those kids—giggling, whispering, staring as if *he* were the one in a costume. Reo dragged his gaze from the motley group to the angel-fairy who led them. She met his look unblinking, her emerald eyes glowing with what could only be amusement. So she thought this was funny, huh? Well, Reo didn't and coolly redirected his gaze to the doors, which slid shut with an ominous thump. At once the elevator began to ascend. Since the woman didn't punch a destination button, he could only assume hers was the same as his: the twenty-third and topmost floor.

Interesting. There was nothing on that floor but Reo's own suite of offices and a large conference room.

"Miz Rusty?" A miniature soldier, who sported camouflage war paint and gear, tugged at the angel-fairy's exotic attire.

The appropriately named Rusty looked down to give the young warrior her full attention. "Yes, Preston?"

"Can we stop on the way and visit my dad?"

"I'm afraid not." Her hair swung when she shook her head. "He's working, you know."

"How about my mommy?" chimed a pint-size princess with big blue eyes and a glitter-encrusted tiara.

"Oh, she is, too, Amy," Rusty assured her. "All your moms and dads are. Sampson Enterprises is a very busy place. We're lucky that the man who owns it is going to let us borrow his conference room for a little while for your Mardi Gras party.''

So that's it, Reo thought. Miz Rusty was no angel or fairy, but one of the workers in the new day care located in the basement of his building. Reo had heard nothing but good about the place since it opened four months ago. According to Angie, his personal assistant and mother of a precocious three-year-old, the children who spent their days there enjoyed a wide range of special celebrations, one of which must be this Mardi Gras party.

Instantly regretting the whim that had prompted him to give in to Angie's pleading and loan out the conference room, Reo imagined how it would look once these rug rats finished with it. The plush beige carpet would never be the same, not to mention the walls and drapes. He closed his eyes and pictured cherry punch spills and chocolate handprints.... It would cost a fortune to have the room cleaned and fumigated.

"It was kind of you to let us share your ride. The elevators have been a nightmare today. I think this one is the only one working."

With a start, Reo realized she talked to him. He felt his face heat. "Er, some kind of electrical glitch, I expect." One definitely deserving of a quick chat with Maintenance...if he could squeeze it in between retrieving the new tuxedo he'd purchased yesterday, then forgotten to take home, and this afternoon's golf game, which he hoped would lead to another sound financial investment.

The redhead nodded and Reo found himself wondering if *Miz* meant Miss, Ms. or Mrs. The sapphire on her third finger, left hand did not solve the mystery since it was mounted on a wide gold band.

"Miz Rusty?" This time it was a sibling of Casper the Friendly Ghost who clamored for the woman's attention. Clearly these children adored their teacher, who appeared to be patience personified, wrapped in a package sexy as hell.

"Yes, Holly?" She straightened the child's costume so that the eyeholes helped instead of hindered her pint-size view.

"Are we almost there? This tickles my tummy."

Miz Rusty laughed. "Mine, too, and, yes, we're almost there." She glanced at the indicator light. "Only seventeen more floors to go."

Thank God, Reo thought, though he had to admit that as children went, this group seemed fairly well behaved. He suspected that Miz Rusty could be thanked for that.

"Only twelve more floors...."

Her voice was easy on the ears—surprisingly deep, a little husky. Seductive with a capital *S*. Reo marveled that such could belong to a woman with freckles dusting her nose. Sexy getup or no, she had a definite tomboy look about her that said she would probably be more at home on a softball field than in his bed.

In his bed?

Reo nearly choked when he realized the inappropriate direction his thoughts had taken. Highly disconcerted, he made a show of pushing his wire-rimmed glasses back up on his nose and straightening the collar of his tasteful paisley golf shirt.

"Just seven more now...."

Her voice also had a pleasant lilt that suggested laughter, Reo realized. He discovered that he actually liked that hint of mischief, that promise of "never a dull moment." How odd. As a rule he preferred predictability in a woman—predictability, independence and intelligence.

"Four, and we're there," *Miz Rusty* announced just as the elevator slammed to a sudden halt and total darkness engulfed them.

The jolt threw Reo forward, but luckily not off his feet. He suspected that some of the children weren't so fortunate. The air instantly resounded with cries and screams of terror, and the elevator rocked in response to frantic scrambling. Reo guessed that Miz Rusty must be surrounded by her panicked charges. Her next words proved it.

"Don't be frightened," she as good as yelled. "Everything's going to be OK."

As if by magic, the auxiliary power kicked in, bathing the enclosure in a dim, reddish glow that did little to soothe Reo's own ruffled composure. Quickly he assessed the damage and saw exactly what he expected: Miz Rusty surrounded by ten clinging youngsters. He reached out and punched the Alarm button, rewarded for his efforts by the sound of a bell ringing loudly somewhere in the bowels of his building.

"See there?" Miz Rusty murmured as she alternately patted, hugged and cajoled each one of them into giving her breathing space. "Everyone knows we're stuck now. I'll bet that this ol' elevator will be moving again in just a second, don't you?" When not one child agreed, she glanced over to Reo, who watched her in silence. "Tell them that this happens all the time," she ordered, words that took a second to soak in.

"Oh, uh, sure. All the time," he then blurted, silently adding, *somewhere* in Shreveport. To his knowledge, today was the first day there had ever been problems with the elevators in *his* building. He wondered fleetingly if their nonstop flight from the fourth floor had been a clue that all was not well with them today, since that was a first, too. Obviously everyone else in this busy building

knew there was an elevator problem today and had utilized the stairs.

"And we'll be moving again in no time, won't we?"

"No time at all," Reo agreed, though he wasn't so
sure.

"See?" Miz Rusty studied the sea of upturned faces
that surrounded her and frowned. "Goodness, you're a
gloomy bunch. May I see some smiles?" She waited a
second, then tried again. "Preston...gimmee a big grin.
Come on now, you can do it...there! Now don't you
feel better? Lauren, you're next. Big smile...yes!"

One by one she talked them into smiling until Reo
suddenly found himself addressed.

"Now it's your turn."

"*Me?*"

"You. I want a great big smile on your face, too, just
like this one." She demonstrated, revealing dimples that
were a sweet surprise.

Reo could only stare, speechless.

With a huff of impatience, Miz Rusty reached out and,
placing the tips of her forefingers at the corners of his
mouth, attempted to help him smile.

Reo, his knees downright wobbly, grudgingly coop-
erated.

"Thanks," Miz Rusty said, for the first time looking
as if she might be a bit ruffled by their situation, too.
But there was only a second's awkward silence before
she turned to her charges and spoke again. "Why don't
we play a game while we wait to get moving? Would
you like that?"

Most of her mesmerized companions nodded. Reo
noted that a smile or two seemed genuine now.

"How about I Spy? Do you like that game?"

More nods. More real smiles.

"OK. I'll go first." Miz Rusty, who was surely an

angel, after all, made a production out of looking all around the elevator. Then she said, "I spy something blue, purple and green, all swirled together."

In spite of himself, Reo could not resist searching the costumes of the children for those three colors "swirled." He didn't find them, but did realize that aside from the soldier, the princess and the ghost, he hadn't a clue as to what these children were dressed up to be. The brunette named Lauren looked as if she'd just stepped out of a harem—an odd choice of costume for a preschooler in his opinion—while one helmeted boy resembled some sort of spaceman or something.

Clearly, Reo was out of touch with the younger set, but he knew that already—from spending most of yesterday on the telephone trying to talk a top clothing designer and her manufacturer husband into joining Sampson Enterprises. There was money to be made in children's wear. He wanted a very large piece of that lucrative pie.

"Danielle's skirt?" guessed a curly headed moppet with sequins on her dress and rhinestones on her earlobes.

Miz Rusty shook her head and smiled. "No, there's no green in it."

"Chris's helmet?"

"No purple or blue in that."

"Katy's skirt?"

Miz Rusty laughed and tossed her hair back over her shoulder. "No blue or green in that. Look again. You can't miss it."

Reo winced in response to a sudden shrill squeal of discovery. At once the harem girl rushed forward and grabbed a handful of his designer shirt. "I found it! I found it!" she exclaimed as she yanked.

In a heartbeat, Miz Rusty stood so close that Reo

could smell her perfume. A wave of intense wanting washed over him as she gently disentangled chubby fingers from the fabric.

"You're right, Lauren. You win!" Smiling an apology, Miz Rusty smoothed his shirt by patting it flat against his chest from collar to belt. "Sorry," she mumbled, before turning her back on him and hustling Lauren back to the others, a matter of three steps.

Reo thanked his lucky stars that she hadn't felt the pounding of his heart through the material. As it was, she could certainly see the pulse dancing in his neck if she so much as glanced his way again. Fortunately, she didn't.

He looked at his watch. How long had they been suspended in time? Ten minutes? Fifteen? It felt like forever, and not because of these harmless kids. No, it was the strain of resisting their sexy keeper, a woman Reo knew instinctively could bring him to his quaking knees.

"Who wants to be next?"

"Let *him,*" replied the child named Danielle, pointing to Reo.

"Yeah," agreed Preston, the soldier.

At once all eyes were on Reo. He felt sweat pop out on his forehead and wished for a cigarette, an amazing development considering he didn't smoke. But on second thought, maybe it was natural. He *did* feel a lot like a prisoner facing a very observant firing squad. He could only pray the pleats in his khaki pants would hide his current state of semiarousal for that firing squad's captivating captain.

"Would you like to play, Mr. um—" Miz Rusty reached out and grasped the clip of the lost-and-found ID badge, protruding from the pocket into which Reo had thoughtlessly tucked it earlier "—Brad Turner of

the mail room?'' She clipped the badge to his collar with
a take-no-prisoners smile.

As disconcerted by Miz Rusty's proximity as he was
insulted by the mistake, Reo didn't bother to correct her.
Instead, he just shook his head. He'd never played I Spy
as a child. Why should he risk it now when his wits had
apparently failed him?

''Please?''

The whispered entreaty gave him goose bumps. *Well
hell.* ''OK. All right.''

Disgruntled, Reo took his sweet time picking out what
he spied. Finally he came to a decision.

''I spy something...red.''

Immediately he was bombarded by guesses—someone's shirt, someone else's vest, shoes or hat. Each time,
Reo shook his head in the negative and instructed them
to ''guess again.'' He took great comfort in the fact that
none of his peers or employees were around to see him
acting the fool for this woman. They respected him. He
didn't want that to change.

''I know! I know!'' It was Princess Amy, hopping
from one foot to the other in the glee of discovery. ''Miz
Rusty's hair!''

''Right!'' Unable to resist, Reo stepped forward and
reached over the children's heads to tug on a long lock
of Miz Rusty's hair, which was as silky soft as he'd
imagined. She blushed—a response that flattered her and
sent his pulse to triple digits—then slapped his hand
away. ''Good for you. Now who wants to be next...?''

Instead of the chorus of *me's* Reo expected, there was
silence that loudly proclaimed impatience to be free.

''No one? Does that mean you want to play a different
game?''

How did she manage her enthusiasm? Reo wondered,
noting her ever-bright smile. He glanced at his watch.

Fifteen minutes they'd been trapped. Fifteen minutes that must seem like fifteen hours to the children and felt like fifteen days to him.

What the hell is wrong with the electricity?

On that very thought the elevator lurched into motion...for maybe half a second. Then it stopped again, so abruptly that one of the costumed children was tossed to the floor. Reo and Miz Rusty moved to rescue him at the same time, soundly bumping heads in the process.

"Ow!"

"Oops!"

Screams of fright became a chorus of laughter that lightened the mood more than I Spy or any other kid's game ever could. Ruefully Reo set the downed child, who wore a goalie mask of all things, back on his feet and assessed him for damages. The boy, who Miz Rusty called Matt, seemed OK.

Obviously taking advantage of the moment, Miz Rusty clapped her hands to get everyone's attention. "Looks like it's going to be another few minutes before we get out of here, so why don't we sing for Brad? Do you know any funny songs?"

They certainly did, and in seconds Reo was treated to a seemingly endless ditty about great green gobs of greasy, grimy gopher guts. The children sang with the enthusiasm and volume of youth. And though Reo's ears soon begged for mercy, he pretended to enjoy the serenade—more uncharacteristic generosity that amazed him. Clearly Miz Rusty's magic was as potent for thirty-five-year-old businessmen as it was for the under-six set, if in a slightly different way.

When that song finally ended, they sang another. And when it ended, others, until a solid hour had passed. Covertly Reo assessed their situation. Plenty of air. Plenty of light—though it flickered threateningly now and then. There wasn't a doubt in his mind that a maintenance crew labored to put the elevator in motion again. He just hoped it didn't take much longer. The mood aboard would surely take a turn for the worst—

"Miz Rusty...Miz Rusty...?"

"What is it, Chad?"

Chad, dressed up like some kind of animal, maybe a bear, tugged her down to his level and then whispered loudly in her ear.

"Can't you hold it?" Miz Rusty whispered back, words that elicited a mental groan from Reo. Here it was...the beginning of the end.

"Maybe," came the not-so-reassuring reply.

"I'm hungry," piped up Chris, the spaceman.

"And I'm thirsty," added Sarah of the sequins and rhinestones.

Miz Rusty's gaze met Reo's across the crowded elevator. She gave him a half smile that could mean anything and then sighed rather lustily. "When we get to the party, there'll be plenty to eat and drink. Meanwhile, did anyone bring any of the candy we gave you earlier?"

If anyone did, they weren't telling.

"I have gum," Reo heard himself blurt, words that resulted in ten new friends...maybe eleven, judging by the relief on Miz Rusty's face.

With great ceremony, Reo withdrew the gum and opened the package. He took out five of the seven pieces and tore each in half. After distributing them to the children, he collected the wrappers and stashed them in a pocket, then shared a sixth piece with Miz Rusty. The other piece he put back in his pocket for an emergency...as if things could get worse.

Miz Rusty accepted the sweet with a smile of gratitude and for several minutes the only sound was melodious smacking. The smell of mint filled the air.

"How about a ghost story?" Reo next heard himself say, an idea that surprised him as much as it did Miz Rusty, who gave him a decidedly doubtful look.

"Don't you think we're, um, *stimulated* enough?"

"Trust me," Reo said, an entreaty she honored with a shrug. He then made everyone, including Miz Rusty, sit in a semicircle and began to recite a time-old story about a less-than-genius grave robber, stolen bones in a box and the ridiculous skeleton who wanted them back. Drawing on memories from one of the few times he was allowed to sleep over with friends as a child, Reo acted out the drama, which ended in a surprise "Boo!" that resulted in squeals and then giggles.

Before the revelry had ceased, the elevator jerked into motion, this time reaching the twenty-second floor before it ground to a halt again. Miz Rusty and Reo reached for the Open Door button at the same time and inadvertently tangled again, resulting in more hilarity.

So it was a joyful group that spilled out of the elevator to be greeted by a maintenance man and two women Reo guessed to be more day-care workers.

"Oh, thank goodness," one of the women exclaimed, reaching out to hug three children at once.

"Are we in time for the party?" Miz Rusty asked, clearly trying to change the subject. Her hint to downplay the event was apparently well taken.

"Of course you are!" the woman exclaimed.

In seconds the children were herded toward the stairs. The wide-eyed maintenance man, who obviously recognized Reo, darted down the hall as if the hounds of hell nipped at his heels—no doubt to report the incident to his boss. That left only Miz Rusty and Reo standing at the foot of the stairs. For a second they just looked at each other without speaking. Reo tried to see past her irresistible girl-next-door charm to the young woman inside. Was she really what she appeared to be—warm and caring with a dash of mischievousness thrown in?

Apparently…and what a contrast to Colleen, a divorce lawyer he'd originally hired to clear up a family mystery and then wound up dating on and off for the past two months. Cold, unless she thought *hot* would better serve her purpose, Colleen had at first seemed to be the woman of Reo's dreams. Then she'd begun to cling and tried to take charge of him.

In retrospect he doubted she'd ever really cared about him as a person, seeing him instead as an asset to her image, a goal to be obtained. As for that mischievous streak so appealing in Miz Rusty…Reo couldn't remember the last time Colleen really smiled. Certainly not this morning, when he refused her demand that they attend tonight's charity ball together.

Reo winced, recalling that ugly, very public scene in the reception area of her law office. Damn, but he was glad he'd finally ditched Counselor Colleen. It felt good to be free again, and he intended to retain that precious freedom for a long time to come.

"You were great," Miz Rusty said, breaking into his memories. Reaching into a pocket hidden by the folds of her gown, she withdrew a tissue that she attempted to dab the sweat still beading on his forehead.

Reo instinctively ducked her touch. "I, um, just followed your lead."

She looked surprised by his action—surprised and a little confused.

"Obviously you're a natural with kids," he added somewhat lamely, unwilling to hurt her, even though he'd just remembered how much he cherished the single life. It wasn't Miz Rusty's fault that she was so sexy. In fact, he doubted that she even knew…which was, of course, part of her appeal.

"Why, thank you."

She studied his expression for a moment as if trying to do some mental probing of her own. Then her lips slowly stretched into what could only be called a hopeful smile, which made Reo wonder if she saw right through his grown-up cool to the lost boy inside.

"What time do you finish up today?" she asked. "I have a meeting right after this party, but after that I'd really like to buy you a beer for being such a good sport on the elevator."

Reo tensed. More times than not when a woman he'd just met got friendly it was a matter of the pocketbook, not the heart. Had she picked up on his attraction to her? Was she now ready to make use of it?

"Brad...?"

Who? Oh, yeah. The alias. Miz Rusty thought he was Brad Turner, a peer, which meant she wasn't after his money at all. How refreshing. So refreshing, in fact, that Reo was very tempted to accept her invitation... vulnerability or no.

Then he remembered he couldn't.

"I have another obligation."

"Oh."

Her smile remained, but he sensed her disappointment.

Reo felt a stab of remorse and, yes, disappointment of his own. At this moment, he realized, there was nothing he'd rather do than spend time with Miz Rusty, who thought he worked in the mail room. They'd find a tavern somewhere where they could drink, dance and get to know each other intimately.

Intimately? He *was* a hormonal wreck! And, it seemed, an idiot, too. What else would one call a man so obviously eager to jump out of that proverbial frying pan into that proverbial fire? Rattled by his apparent dim wits, Reo quickly changed the subject. "Are you, um, supposed to be Tinkerbell?"

She shook her head. "Guess again."

"An angel?"

Miz Rusty bubbled with incredulous laughter. "Not by a long shot."

At that softly drawled promise, Reo's brain shut down for good, leaving him a babbling victim of desire. "I—I give up then. What are you?"

"A witch," she whispered, her mouth quite close to his ear as if she feared someone else might overhear, even though they were now too, too alone.

Reo put his hands in his pockets to keep from touching her hair, her cheek, her— "But witches wear black."

"Only the bad ones. I'm good."

I'll bet you are. Shivering as if someone's fingertips had traced a path up his spine, he could not resist asking, "What, exactly, do good witches do?"

"Why, good things, of course."

Her eyes twinkled with mischief. Her smile had returned full force. He could tell she enjoyed this foolish exchange as much as he—God help him. "Can you please be more specific?"

"More specific... Hmmm. Well, good witches cast good spells."

"Yeah? What else?"

"They break bad ones."

"And?..."

"They mix love potions."

Something *she'd* never need, Reo realized, since that wicked smile of hers was all it took to turn one of the city's most savvy businessmen—namely *him*—into a libidinous lunatic.

Time to get the hell out of the Sampson Building.

"Rusty? Are you coming?" The words wafted down the stairs from somewhere above, startling them both.

"Be right there," Miz Rusty called back, much to Reo's relief. "Now I want you to repeat after me—"

"What? Why?"

"Just do it, OK?"

Reo nodded cautiously.

"Five, five, five…"

"Five, five, five…" he muttered, so dazed that he hadn't a clue as to where she was headed.

"Six, three, seven, seven."

"Six, three, seven, sev—" Her phone number! She was giving him her phone number! Damn. "Six, three, seven, seven."

"Good. Now say it again so I can be sure you have it right."

"Five, five, five, six, three, seven, seven." He'd always been a whiz with numbers—a blessing until now.

"Perfect," Miz Rusty said, adding, "And remember…my offer to buy you a beer has no expiration date." With a wave she moved quickly away from him, her skirt billowing out behind.

It took Reo several seconds to recover from the rain check, and by then she'd reached the midpoint landing and disappeared from view. She took with her the sunshine, leaving him in the shadow that was his life these days. Disgusted, disoriented and apparently as weak in the head as the knees, Reo stood looking after her for a moment. Then he slowly turned and trailed the maintenance man down the hall.

Chapter Two

"Chin up. Shoulders back. Stomach in. Chest out."

"*Chest out!*" Beatrice Hanson, dubbed "Rusty" at birth by her older sister, snorted her opinion of that ridiculous order and tugged up the strapless bodice of the evening dress her housemate, Jade Martinelli, had rented for her to wear to tonight's charity ball. Tight, black and sequined, it boasted a neck cut halfway to her belly button. Rusty felt naked. "I'll have you know that if my chest sticks out any farther than it already does, I'm going to be arrested for indecent exposure."

"Not tonight," her friend replied, eyeing Rusty's shiny finery in the full-length mirror before which the two of them stood. "Tonight you'll fit right in *and* turn the head of every rich bachelor in the place—exactly what *I'm* hoping to do. And to think you're only going to this shindig to make some business contacts." She sighed as if Rusty were crazy or, at the least, a lost cause.

For a second they stared at their reflections in silence—two young women so opposite in looks, personality and motives, yet both dressed to knock 'em dead. Rusty suddenly wished she hadn't let Jade talk her into tonight's glitzy affair, even though it would be an excellent opportunity to rub elbows with some well-to-do moms more than willing to let someone like Rusty plan their children's elaborate parties.

"Thanks for agreeing to go with me on such short notice," Jade said, as if picking up on Rusty's regrets.

"How could I refuse when you bribed me with a free ticket, free dress *and* free manicure." Rusty held out her hands and inspected the bright crimson polish applied at a nail boutique barely an hour ago. "What do you think of the color?"

"Snazzy. Hides the red punch stain under your fingernails."

Rusty grimaced at the truth of that. Such stains were an occupational hazard when one hosted children's parties for a living. Lemon juice worked beautifully to remove the unwanted tint…when she found time to use it. She'd been busy until four o'clock today with a Mardi Gras celebration at the Sampson Enterprises day care, then had a very productive meeting with Angie Mallett, mother of one of the kids and a personal assistant to the CEO of the company.

"Are you ready to go? I'm dying to make an entrance." Jade tucked a stray strand of her luxurious dark hair into the curls pinned up tonight to reveal faux diamond earrings. She wore scarlet, and if Rusty's dress could be called *indecent,* Jade's should be called *illegal.* Rusty knew that when bachelor heads turned, it would not be to look at a five-foot-five, freckle-faced redhead playing dress up. No, Jade, six feet tall and dark, would catch the eye of every man in the room, just as she

always did. And who knew…maybe this time one of
them would actually meet her mercenary standards.

"I'm ready," answered Rusty, who held no malice
toward Jade for her misguided goals. Tonight Rusty's
could only be considered fiscal, too. She'd been trying
for ages to extend her client base to the influential side
of town. This glitzy fund-raiser was just the social opportunity she needed. Rusty had high hopes for the evening, knowing things could only get better.

"We'll take my car," Jade said, breaking into Rusty's
thoughts.

"You mean you didn't hire a golden carriage, oh
Fairy Godmother?"

Jade hooted with laughter. "Cinderella, you ain't."

"And neither are you," Rusty said, a gentle reminder
that sobered the effervescent Jade for maybe half a second.

"Look…just because a rich guy dumped on your sister is no reason to assume they're all jerks. In fact, I'm
more than willing to give one a whirl." She shrugged
and led the way to the door. "Who knows? Maybe I'll
even get lucky tonight. Heck, honey, maybe you will,
too." She stopped short, a faraway look in her eye. "I
can see it all now. You walk into the ballroom, nothing
on your mind but business. You make a beeline for the
first mommy-type you see, only to stop short when a
strange man catches your eye. He's tall, he's dark, he's
handsome, he's rich. Most important, he's instantly in
love with you."

"Good grief, Jade. Would you quit talking nonsense
and come on?"

"You're drawn to him like metal to a magnet."

"We're going to be late."

"Time stands still as the two of you come together,

embrace and…kiss." The last word was little more than a sigh.

"Are you coming or not?" Rusty tapped her toe on the floor in impatience.

"Suddenly it's hearts, flowers and forever after."

"Jade, I'm warning you…"

"And you never have to worry about anything again." Jade's eyes glazed.

"Snap out of it!"

It took several seconds, but Jade's stare finally focused, and with a heavy sigh, she shrugged her acceptance of cold reality and once again headed for the door. "Can I help it if I'm a hopeful romantic and you're a hopeless stick-in-the-mud?"

"Stick-in-the-mud!" Rusty stopped short. "I'll have you know I'm the hostess with the mostest."

"To the under-five set, maybe," Jade answered, stopping to look back at her.

Rusty's jaw dropped. "Are you saying I don't know how to act around adults?"

"Yes, and male adults in particular."

"I'll have you know that I offered to buy a beer for a very handsome guy this very afternoon. I even gave him my phone number."

"You're kidding! Who?"

"His name is Brad Turner. He works in the mail room at Sampson."

"You tried to pick up a teenager?"

"He was much older than that. Probably in his mid- to late-thirties."

"God, Rusty. Only you would hit on a thirty-year-old mail clerk. That's an entry position in any company. He's got to be a real dud to still be in that sort of job at thirty."

"So maybe he's a supervisor or something," murmured Rusty, somewhat defensively. Trust Jade to find something wrong with a man who would've knocked Rusty's socks off earlier that day...had she been wearing any. As it was, he'd made her poor ol' heart thump like a tom-tom.

She closed her eyes, remembering just how he looked: shaggy dark hair, gorgeous baby blues, chiseled jawline shadowed by whiskers no amount of shaving could completely erase. The man's body was nothing to scoff at, either, as she recalled. Muscular...obviously fit. So what if he was a bit slow to warm up? He'd become quite human before their elevator time came to an end. And if she'd just had another half hour with him, he might even have loosened up enough to accept her offer of a beer.

"I'll bet you a dollar to a doughnut he's *not* a supervisor," said Jade, bursting into Rusty's Technicolor memories. "Want to know how I know?"

"Not really, but I'm sure you're going to tell me, anyway."

"I know because you have no taste in men. I mean, give you a lineup of nine blue-ribbon bachelors and one nerd, and *you'll* pick the nerd every time."

"Brad was not a nerd, Jade. He was a nice man. *Nice* is important—more important, in fact, than a hefty bank balance." Rusty shook her head, searching for words to describe the incredible feelings Brad had evoked. "What can I say? He just knocked me out."

"Heaven help me," Jade murmured, throwing up her hands in exasperation and stepping out her front door.

Hesitating for a heartbeat, then following on Jade's heels, Rusty silently echoed that sentiment. It would take all the angels in heaven plus a few here on earth to get her through this night's gathering of high society without making a fool of herself.

Just half an hour later the two women stood outside the shiny brass doors of an elite country club. Following her friend's lead, Rusty handed a uniformed doorman her gold-embossed ticket and stepped into fairyland. At least, that's what it felt like, thanks to half a dozen enormous crystal chandeliers that illuminated the vast hall.

Pausing just inside the door with Jade at her side, Rusty scanned the crowded room for a familiar face and immediately saw several—the mayor of the city, standing next to the governor of the state, a U.S. senator, a local television talk-show host and a well-known brain surgeon. Not the crowd she usually ran with, Rusty realized, instantly abandoning all plans to peddle her paltry parties. Judging from the diamonds and furs in this room, any one of these mothers could simply rent Disneyland if they wanted to throw an extra-special birthday bash.

Thank goodness that afternoon's appointment with Angie Mallett had gone so well. If their business arrangement worked out as discussed, Rusty would soon have one heck of a reference for her résumé, and a lack of contacts tonight really wouldn't be the end of the world.

"I think we're out of our league, here," Rusty murmured to Jade, more than a little curious how her lower-middle-class housemate had wrangled invitations to this *upper*-upper-class event.

When Jade did not reply, Rusty looked around to discover that she now stood alone.

"Great," she muttered in dismay, searching the crowd for her flashy friend, who was not to be found.

Though half-tempted to turn tail and run, Rusty squared her shoulders instead and began to wind her way through the crush of people, destination unknown. She said nothing to anyone, barely risking a timid smile, and that only when someone else smiled first.

It would be easy to turn into a wallflower tonight instead of working the room, she decided, now near hyperventilation point. How nice to stand safely to one side of the room, watching the posturing of the filthy rich.

"Well, if it isn't Miz Rusty…"

Astonished to hear someone—especially a male someone—speaking her name, Rusty whirled around.

"Mail room Brad! Gosh, it's good to see you." It was all she could do not to hug the man—a virtual stranger, who at this moment was as welcome as a long-lost friend.

"I didn't know you were going to be here," Brad murmured, stepping so close that she had to tip her head back to meet his gaze. Rusty noted that he looked as astonished to see her as she was to see him.

"Neither did I," she answered, laughing, oh so thrilled to see someone in her price range…especially *this* someone. "Is this—" she swept her arms to encompass the room "—the 'obligation' you mentioned earlier today?"

Brad nodded in reply, his gaze frisking Rusty from head to toe.

"Do this sort of thing often?" Rusty next asked, intrigued. Clearly Jade wasn't the only peasant with impressive social connections.

"Only when I have to," he said.

Rusty smiled at that and made an appraisal of her own, beginning at Brad's satin bow tie and gradually encompassing his cummerbund, snow-white shirt, and perfectly tailored black jacket and pants. And to think she'd thought him gorgeous in khaki. He seemed so relaxed, too. As if he wore this kind of getup all the time.

The strangest feeling of uneasiness sneaked up on Rusty, who didn't understand, so ignored it. What was surely going to be the worst night of her life had just turned into the best. Brad was here, and for all his cool demeanor hadn't once looked away from her shiny black dress.

Warming up in response to his heated stare, Rusty asked, "Is there a punch bowl close by?"

"I believe there is, yes." He stood tall enough to look over most heads, so did. "I see it. Are you thirsty?"

"Dry as the Sahara."

"Then allow me to get you a drink." He stepped away, only to stop short when Rusty reached out and grabbed his arm.

"I'm coming, too," she announced, slipping a hand into his. If the familiarity surprised Brad, he covered it well and led the way to a buffet table heaped with artfully presented hors d'oeuvres, fruits, desserts and, best of all, drinks.

Brad moved to the punch bowl, supervised the filling of a crystal cup, then handed it to Rusty, who gratefully swallowed the entire contents. Alcoholic? she wondered, savoring the tangy flavor. Perhaps one of those drinks that hit hard later, scrambling the wits of unsuspecting young women when they least expected it? Why, by midnight she might find herself at Brad's mercy—inhibitions gone with the wind.

Rusty choked back a laugh that threatened to spew what was probably only ginger ale and fruit juice. Instinct told her that Brad wasn't the sort of guy who'd take advantage of a woman, even if attracted to her. And as far as Rusty could tell, he wasn't all that attracted beyond a typical male interest in her female anatomy, a good bit of which showed at the moment.

In fact, he seemed really uneasy, and just then his gaze was everywhere but on her dress. Did he, perhaps, have a date waiting for him somewhere in this huge room? A date who now tapped her foot in impatience and wondered where in the heck he'd gone?

"Am I keeping you from someone?"

That got his attention again. "What? Oh, um, no. Why?"

"You seem so...restless."

"Sorry. It's just that I'm never really comfortable at functions such as this."

"Then why'd you come?"

"I'd promised," Brad replied with a shrug. "Besides, it's for a good cause. Don't you agree?"

"Oh, sure." Rusty, who didn't even know what cause that was, felt her face heat. At that moment Brad's gaze found her gown again. He looked at it so long she felt her face get even hotter and had to wonder if he had X-ray vision. Suddenly she felt smothered. "What's beyond those doors?"

"A veranda."

"Perfect," Rusty muttered, handing her empty glass to a waiter with a tray and then heading straight for some nearby French doors, half-hidden behind diaphanous white curtains.

With a twist of the knob, they swung open. She stepped outside onto what turned out to be a wide balcony. The air, unusually warm for late February, felt heavenly and smelled that way, too, thanks to the winter rose garden just beyond. Colorful and fragrant, it lured

Rusty, and without hesitation she negotiated a stairway descent and entered it.

"Now this is more like it," she murmured to herself as she sniffed a perfect red rose.

"So you hate crowds, too?"

Rusty spun around to find that Brad had followed and now stood right behind her. She really hadn't expected that. "Some crowds. Certainly this one."

"What's wrong with this one?"

His tone hinted he might be offended. Rusty arched an eyebrow in surprise. "Why, it's too ritzy, of course."

"You expected something else?" Now he sounded bemused.

"As a matter of fact I did, probably because my housemate Jade Martinelli, who provided my ticket, is so normal."

"Jade Martinelli?" He said the name slowly and softly as if vaguely familiar with it. Rusty hoped he hadn't read it on a bathroom wall somewhere.

"That's right. Um...do you know her?"

"I'm not sure." He hesitated a millisecond longer, then gave it up with a shake of his head. "So you think that the people in that room aren't as *normal* as you and your friend, Jade?"

"If normal is based on most citizens of this country, then I'd have to say no. Based on my experience, people who have this much money are ridiculously preoccupied with making more and don't realize what's really important in life." Belatedly, she noted Brad's frown. "Not that some of the people in there aren't nice," she quickly added. "I mean they're here supporting this charity, aren't they?"

He nodded. "Yes, and at considerable cost to them."

Considerable cost? Just how much was that? Rusty

wondered, trying in vain to ignore a second stab of uneasiness. What on earth had Jade hocked to get the money for their tickets? Her soul? Rusty gulped. Surely not her body. "I'm thinking we should talk about something else."

"Not until we sit down," Brad answered, looking a bit relieved. "Then we can talk about whatever you want."

He looked around, spotted an ornate wrought-iron bench several yards farther into the garden, and led the way as they maneuvered through the flowers to get to it. Rusty seated herself beside him...or tried to. Her shoes slipped on the dew-kissed grass, resulting in an abrupt descent that put her half on and half off the bench. Luckily Brad had quick reflexes and saved her from landing on her butt on the ground. Not so luckily, his hand bumped her right breast, which nearly popped completely out of the dress.

"Sorry," he murmured, face crimson even in the dim glow of the countless twinkle lights illuminating the garden.

"That's OK," Rusty replied, turning her back on him, tugging the dress back up. "Mind if I slip off these shoes? They're lethal on this wet grass."

"Go right ahead."

An awkward silence settled on them as she stepped out of the strappy black shoes and set them to one side. The dew felt great on her tortured soles, and Rusty couldn't help but wiggle her cramped toes as she slid back onto the bench and gave Brad a self-conscious smile. Belatedly she noticed that his arm lay on the back of the bench and now kept her bare skin from touching the cool metal.

Disconcerted, Rusty cleared her throat rather noisily.

"So, um, how long have you worked at Sampson, Brad?"

"Nineteen years."

Rusty's jaw dropped. "They hire toddlers?"

"I started in the mail room at sixteen," Brad told her with a grin.

So he was thirty-five—older than she'd expected, but only seven years more than her own twenty-eight.

"How long have you been working with kids?" he then asked.

"Six years. I was a secretary before that. Hated putting on panty hose every day, so knew I had to find another line of work." She heard the echo of her candid admission and tensed. "Guess you didn't need to know that last bit of trivia."

"Actually," Brad answered with a laugh so sexy it made her palms sweat, "it gives me a whole new view of you...not that there's anything wrong with the current one." His gaze swept her from head to toe, just as it had earlier that night. "Did I tell you how beautiful you look?"

"Why, no." She couldn't prevent her smile of pleasure. "Did I tell you how handsome *you* look?"

"No." He smiled back.

Rusty felt magic in the air—sheer magic that was three parts romance and one part sex. She desperately wanted him to kiss her, and, when he didn't right away, swayed ever so slightly in his direction to encourage him.

Brad took the hint. Swiftly eliminating the space between them, he covered her lips with his in a kiss so all-consuming that her head actually spun, and time, place, *everything else but him* receded into black.

His mouth moved seductively over hers; his fingers

brushed over her bare shoulders, then slid down her arms. Rusty shivered in anticipation of where he might touch next, all the while doing a little digital exploration of her own—his rugged jawline, his broad shoulders, the crisp cotton barrier of the shirt covering his chest.

She wished time could stand still. That she and Brad could spend forever—or at least another hour—all alone in this aromatic garden with beautiful music playing softly inside the building.

"Rusty? Are you out here?"

It was Jade...damn the luck. And even as Rusty considered ignoring the hissed words, Brad abruptly ended the kiss.

"I think I heard someone call your name."

"My friend, Jade." Reluctantly Rusty stood. "I'll just go see what she wants. Shouldn't take but a second."

"Then I'll wait right here."

Good...no, *excellent,* she decided as she left him and slipped, shoeless, back through the flowers to the veranda. There stood Jade, clearly agitated.

"What are you doing out here all alone?" she instantly demanded, her voice breathless and low. "I've been looking for you for at least thirty minutes."

Rusty grinned. "Actually, I'm not alone."

"Oh, my God," Jade exclaimed, grabbing Rusty's arm in a painful clench. "Are you with *him?*"

"Him who?"

"The guy I saw you with at the buffet table. The one who gave you a cup of punch."

"That's exactly who I'm with, and you'll never, ever guess who he is."

"I don't have to guess," Jade said. "I know. He's Reo Sampson, CEO of Sampson Enterprises."

Rusty hooted with laughter at that ridiculous statement. "He is not, silly. His name is Brad Turner...the very same Brad I offered to buy a beer for this afternoon. Remember my telling you about the mail room guy?"

Jade shook her head and began to drag Rusty toward the door. "I don't know any Brad. I do know that the man I saw you with a while ago is Reo Sampson, former boyfriend of Colleen O'Shaunessy, my boss."

Rusty dug her stockinged heels into the veranda, bringing them both to an abrupt halt. "You're confused."

"No, darling, *you* are," Jade retorted, once again tugging on Rusty's arm. "And that means we've got to get out of here and quick." They were at the French doors now. Jade glanced back toward the garden, gasped as if she'd seen a ghost, then lunged through the doorway, pulling Rusty along behind. Spinning, she shut and locked the door.

"What on earth are y—" Rusty tripped on her dress, too long now that she'd abandoned the high heels. Torn between retrieving her shoes and following Jade, Rusty stood frozen in indecision. Jade, however, never looked back as she rapidly circumvented the crowd of guests by keeping to the walls. With a huff of exasperation, Rusty came to an abrupt decision and scurried after her.

In seconds they reached an exit, both breathless. Jade yanked open the door and slipped outside, once again hauling Rusty after her. Only when the heavy door clicked shut behind them did the brunette pause for breath, stepping past Rusty to sag against the brick building, squashing her bare toe in the process.

"Ow!" Rusty raised the hem of her skirt and peered down at her foot, fully expecting to find the toe smashed to smithereens.

"Where are your shoes?"

"Back in the garden with Brad."

"His name is not Brad. It's Reo. Reo Sampson."

Rusty studied Jade, noting that she seemed as sincere as she was out of breath. "You're really sure?"

"Of course I'm sure. I saw the man just this morning in O'Shaunessy's reception room. They were fighting because he wouldn't go with her to the fund-raiser."

"What fund-raiser?"

"*This* fund-raiser."

"And was the fight just a silly fuss or were they really angry with each other?"

"They *ended their professional and personal relationships* before my eyes, Rusty. What do you think?" Jade sounded a little put out at Rusty for her curiosity.

Rusty didn't care. She had to be sure she hadn't just kissed some other woman's man. "So why would Brad, er, Reo lie to me about his identity?"

"I'm afraid it might have something to do with me."

"What?"

"Look, Rusty. We really need to go."

"But—"

"I can see the car from here. If we cut through that flower bed—"

"I'm barefoot!"

"And climb that fence—"

"In this gown?"

"We'll be outta here in no time!" That said, the ever-athletic Jade hiked up her skirt past her knees and loped across the grass to a flower bed, through which she plunged without hesitation and without consideration for the poor landscaper who'd surely labored for days to make it look so pretty.

Rusty stared after her in disbelief for maybe a heartbeat before she, too, lifted the hem of her skirt and dashed across the lawn.

Jade owed her answers. Rusty intended to get them.

Panting by the time they reached the car, Jade jabbed her key in the lock, swung open the door and slipped behind the wheel. With a click of a switch, she unlocked the passenger door.

"Hurry!" she ordered even as Rusty dropped into the seat.

Seconds later, tires squealed as Jade drove out of the lot.

"Talk," Rusty demanded as soon as they lost sight of the country club.

"I can't talk and drive."

"Since when?"

"Since tonight," Jade snapped, shaking her head, then adding, "Oh, God, what a mess. Why did this have to happen?"

"What, exactly, has happened?"

Jade shifted her eyes from the road and gave Rusty a long, appraising look. "If I tell you the truth, will you still be my friend?"

Rusty, who hadn't heard those words since the two of them were grade school buddies, winced. "Oh, Jade, is it that bad?" Jade had always had a knack for getting into mischief.

Jade nodded.

Rusty sighed and responded with her part of the litany. "You'll be my friend forever." *Even if you did sell your body to buy tonight's tickets.*

"I think Reo Sampson knows I fished our fund-raiser tickets out of Colleen O'Shaunessy's trash."

"Excuse me?"

It was Jade's turn to sigh. "When Reo Sampson and

my boss had their fight this morning, she threw the two tickets she'd bought for this party into her wastebasket. As soon as they cleared out of the room, I rescued the tickets.''

"Oh, Jade, you didn't.''

"This is *the* social event of the year, Rusty. I've always wanted to attend. She obviously didn't. Why waste the tickets?''

"How much did she pay for them?''

"A thousand dollars each.''

"Ach!''

"Yeah, but she can afford it. Heck, she pays that much for her hair barrettes.''

"That's not the point. You stole those tickets. We went to that fund-raiser under false pretenses.''

"And Reo Sampson is aware of it. I'm going to lose my job. I just know it, and you can certainly forget the man ever calling you for a date.''

Just my luck, Rusty thought. Then logic waved a red flag before her eyes. "Wait…how could he possibly suspect you took the tickets?''

"He's no idiot, Rusty. He watched me watch *her* throw the tickets in the waste can. He's well aware I could never afford to pay for even one of them and probably even saw the greedy gleam in my eye. Two trashed tickets. Me and you appearing at his party—''

"*His* party?''

"Well, not literally, but he does donate big bucks to this charity and attends this fund-raiser every year. I'm certain he has a say in who's invited. He surely knows you and I were not on the list.''

"How could you have thought for one second that you'd get away with this, Jade Martinelli? I mean, you *knew* the man was going to be here. Didn't it occur to you that he might see you, recognize you, *wonder how in the hell you got in the door?*''

"You don't understand. I heard him tell O'Shaunessy that he had other plans tonight. How was I supposed to know he just meant he preferred going to this thing stag instead of with her?"

"Use your head, Jade. Your boss was undoubtedly trying to impress Reo by buying tickets to an event he always attends. When he refused to accompany her, she knew they were through—the reason for the fight."

"Oh." Jade began to chew on her bottom lip, a little-girl expression of angst that had survived her childhood. "I'm sorry, OK? I never thought…"

And that, of course, was the problem. Jade never did think. Probably never would. Rusty held up a hand, halting what was surely going to be a nonstop flow of apologies that would not even be heard by the man who needed to hear it. Meanwhile, he undoubtedly thought she was partner to Jade's crime.

So much for romance with a good-looking mail clerk. And so much for romance with a good-looking rich man. If he ever dialed the phone number she'd given him it would be a miracle.

Not that she even wanted him to now. Rusty knew first- and secondhand about rich businessmen who, when they weren't having affairs with close friends' wives, spent way too much time at the office getting richer. Hadn't she just witnessed the heartbreak of her very own sister, once married to a man who'd risen from clerk to company president? "Damn!"

Jade nearly ran off the road at the sound of Rusty's blurted curse. Successfully startled into silence, she glanced hesitantly over at her passenger, who now floundered in the wave of yet another ramification to tonight's folly.

Come Monday, Rusty was scheduled to meet with Angie Mallett's boss at Sampson Enterprises to finalize the business arrangements for the most exciting—and lucrative—assignment of her life.

And just who was Angie's boss?

Why, the CEO of that company…none other than *Reo Sampson* himself!

Chapter Three

Alone in his study, Reo Sampson sat at the massive desk that once belonged to his maternal grandfather and frowned at the pair of women's shoes he held, one in each hand. They were high heels—strappy, black numbers with 7 1/2 M imprinted on the inside.

Foolish shoes worn by a mystery woman he'd met mere hours ago on an elevator and could not seem to forget.

She called herself Rusty. Her eyes were green. Her figure could keep a man up all night—Reo grinned at his pun—wondering what it would be like to love her.

Love her? Oh no, not that. Never that.

Make love to her? Much more like it, since his crazy, undeniable attraction to Rusty was fleeting and physical—nothing more. How could it be when she was so flighty, a trait he abhorred in anyone? There were other traits that made her unsuitable for romantic pursuit, Reo assured himself, well aware that if unpredictability were her only fault, his body might yet win over his common sense, and he might dial the phone number he'd unwittingly put to memory.

Knowing he thought best on paper, he reached for a piece of stationery embossed with the company logo and an ink pen, the kind that used real ink from a bottle and produced bold, black strokes. Laying the paper on the desk, he drew a line from the top of the page to the bottom. The left column he labeled "Know"; the right, he labeled "Don't Know."

Reo then began to list exactly what he could or couldn't say for certain about Miz Rusty, so that he could discourage what he believed could become a full-blown obsession with her. Under "Know" he wrote "hair color, eye color, shoe size, profession, phone number, name...." Here Reo paused. Unless *Miz* were her first name and *Rusty* her last, he didn't know her name at all. Besides that, "Rusty" had to be a nickname based on hair color. Reo shook his head, wondering exactly how he and this unnamed woman wound up together in the garden at Ten Oaks Country Club, sharing one hot kiss.

Things had moved much too fast since the moment they met yesterday. And he had a funny feeling that the two of them might have shared more than just a kiss last night if her friend Jade hadn't suddenly appeared and dragged her away.

Jade. Frowning, Reo wrote something else under "Know": "Shares house with woman named Jade."

Now why did that name—and the statuesque brunette to whom it belonged—seem so familiar? he wondered, even as he visualized a nameplate on a desk in an office in which he'd been more than once.

"Well, hell!" Reo suddenly exclaimed, slapping his palm to his forehead. Obviously Witch Rusty had put a spell on him. Why else would he not realize at once that Jade—a woman who dressed like an expensive but classy hooker, flirted shamelessly with all male clients and typed faster than humanly possible—worked for Colleen O'Shaunessy.

Jade had also not only witnessed his uncivilized split with Colleen, but *knew* his real name. At once Reo felt foolish for not having told Rusty the truth the first time she'd called him Brad. He had his reasons, of course, not the least of which was the novelty of being appreciated for something besides his money.

Was his real identity, then, the reason Miz Rusty had run last night? Reo hoped not. The idea that she'd run *from* instead of *to* when she learned who he was thoroughly intrigued him. He could feel his curiosity piquing, and he ruthlessly squashed it by reminding himself that the reason she'd fled was undoubtedly because Jade had told her about Colleen.

But no...Jade, who'd watched the fight, knew Reo and the lawyer were no longer a pair, knew he was free to kiss any woman he wanted.

Reo sighed his frustration. Second-guessing a female was pretty darned tricky—not a skill at which he excelled. He honestly couldn't think of a single good reason why Jade would warn Rusty away...unless...unless Colleen O'Shaunessy had shared confidential information about his grandfather's possible indiscretion.

Such a scandal might put Rusty off, Reo realized. And God only knew Colleen desperately wanted to keep her skillful receptionist in her employ. Why, that fork-tongued lawyer had probably gone right back out in the reception area after Reo's departure and lambasted the Sampson name. As a result, Jade had simply tried to save Rusty, a friend, from a fate worse than death.

Yeah. That was it.

Pleased to have figured that out, Reo stared at the column labeled "Know" for maybe half a minute more. Coming up blank, he then shifted his gaze to the other column, the one labeled "Don't know." Under this heading, he first wrote "address," then proceeded to fill up the entire half of the page.

After several minutes of nonstop writing, Reo tossed down the pen in thorough disgust. How could he—a man who weighed even the smallest decisions as if they were life impacting—have held Rusty so tight? Kissed her so hard? Wanted her so badly?

She was a stranger, for crying out loud. A woman about whom he knew nothing that really mattered. A woman he couldn't forget.

Thank God for Jade, who'd so conveniently filled Rusty's head with Colleen's lies. Their flight from the charity ball proved that they thought him a growly beast best avoided.

Beast? Reo laughed aloud and without humor. Wrong fairy tale, he realized, picking up one of Rusty's shoes and eyeing it. Although a beautiful woman, Rusty wasn't Beauty, but Cinderella, which made him Prince Charming. Yet Rusty believed he was anything but charming—the reason she'd run.

Should he reveal his true nature? Don the role of the fabled prince and scour the countryside for the fair maiden whose foot fit the shoe? Not by a long shot, Reo decided. Not only was he no Prince Charming, this particular maiden was too dangerous, too powerful, too beautiful—a woman who fascinated him, a woman he could not resist.

And why go to that much trouble, anyway? All he

really had to do was dial the number she'd given him, a number lodged firmly in his memory.

Snatching up the telephone, Reo impulsively pulled the plug and stashed the instrument in the top-right desk drawer, which he slammed shut. He stared at the drawer for a second, then reached into another drawer to retrieve a small key, which he inserted into a lock and twisted, thereby securing the entire desk. Not feeling safe just yet, however, Reo next dropped the key into a bud vase, which he set on the top shelf of his bookcase.

Saved, he thought, at least for the moment.

As for later...well, a good night's sleep would work wonders to erase Rusty from his heart and head. With luck—and careful avoidance of the Sampson Enterprises Day Care—he'd never see her again.

So what if a million questions about her remained unanswered? He could handle not knowing the answers. Hell, he was Reo Sampson, overworked CEO of one of the largest business conglomerates in the state.

He could handle anything.

The ring of the phone summoned Rusty from the shower at nine-thirty on Monday morning. She instantly assumed that the very worst had happened. Reo Sampson had somehow figured out what Jade had done and made the connection between Jade and Rusty. He'd then discovered that Rusty and the woman his assistant had found to entertain the children of potential out-of-town clients during contract negotiations were one and the same. Angie, of course, was now calling to cancel the deal....

"Hello?"

"Rusty, it's Jade."

"What'd you forget?" Rusty asked with a sigh of

relief, wrapping the towel around her bare body and sitting on the edge of her bed.

"Bandit. I let him outside this morning, but didn't let him back in." Jade referred to the mixed-breed pup that she and Rusty had rescued from the pound a few months ago and both adored. "Now it's raining. Would you please get him in from the wet?"

"Either he opened the door himself," Rusty said, reaching out to pat the head of the mutt in question, who grinned—at least that's what Rusty called that particular expression. "Or you did it and don't remember."

"Oh. Well, that's good." There was a long silence. "Um…have you heard anything from that Angie lady at Sampson?"

Guessing that this was the real reason for the call, Rusty graciously set Jade's mind at rest. "No, so everything must be fine."

"Gosh, I hope so. Call me when you get back from the interview, OK? I want to hear everything Reo Sampson has to say about Friday night."

Well, I don't, Rusty silently replied, aloud saying only, "All right. How's it gone with you so far, by the way?"

"O'Shaunessy hasn't said a thing, so she must not know what I did."

"You're very lucky."

"You can say that again," Jade agreed with a heartfelt sigh before hanging up the phone.

Rusty sat for several seconds after, dreading what the day might hold. To her way of thinking, there was simply no way Reo Sampson could hire her, once he realized she'd crashed the fund-raiser. Not that it was such a huge crime. It really wasn't any worse than his not telling her his real name the first time she'd called him Brad. Rusty still wondered about that, but not often, since she had more important problems clouding her thoughts at the moment.

One of those problems was the fact that Angie Mallett had stressed how particular the would-be clients of Reo Sampson were. Obviously no woman with character or an ounce of class would sneak into a charity ball the way Rusty had done. She could only hope her foolish mistake would not compromise her chances at this job she wanted so badly.

Promptly at ten-thirty, Rusty stepped off the elevator on the twenty-third floor of the Sampson Enterprises building. It worked beautifully today, rising to the top of the modern structure without so much as a bump, jolt or pause. Half wishing she was stuck between floors somewhere, Rusty straightened the collar of her crisp, white blouse and tugged at the jacket sleeves of her navy blue power suit.

She'd dressed for success. She could only hope it helped.

"Why, hello, Beatrice," Angie Mallett greeted her moments later in the reception room.

Rusty winced at the sound of her given name. "I go by 'Rusty,' remember? No one but the grandmother I'm named after dares call me Beatrice."

"I forgot." Angie, a vivacious blonde with a friendly smile, laughed. "Are you ready to meet Mr. Sampson?"

"Sure," Rusty answered, a lie. If she never saw the man again, it would be too soon.

Motioning for Rusty to follow, Angie led the way into a plush office. Rusty saw Reo at once, sitting at a huge desk, his chair swiveled around to face a row of windows so that his back faced her. He had a telephone to his ear and appeared to be deeply engrossed in conversation, a fact for which Rusty was grateful since it gave her a second to look him over before the eggs hit the fan.

Same dark hair. Same thick neck, wide shoulders, long arms.

Lord, but the man was still gorgeous. Rusty's heart began to thump erratically. Her knees, to quake.

"Why don't you have a seat," Angie whispered, indicating chairs across the desk from her boss. "I think he's winding down."

Grateful for the timely offer, Rusty sank into the one farthest from Reo. Angie took the other. Seconds ticked by.

"It's dinner tonight, then," Reo suddenly said, swiveling around to face Angie. Focused solely on the problem at hand—a masculine trait Rusty usually found annoying, but appreciated today—he pulled a leather-bound pocket calendar out of his pocket and slid it across the desk to his assistant, seated directly in front of him, poised pen in hand. "Sartoni's at eight. I look forward to seeing you both." Reo dropped the receiver in the cradle and raised his gaze to Angie, in whom he obviously placed much confidence. "Did you get that down?"

"Actually, you have a conflict. You're supposed to dine with Edward Logan Stiles tonight."

"Who?"

"The New Orleans lawyer you've hired to replace Miss O'Shaunessy."

"Oh, yeah. Reschedule him for tomorrow night, will you? The Moreaus want to meet with me and Miss, um—" he glanced at a piece of paper on his desk "—Hanson as soon as possible."

Uh-oh. Certain that a shift in focus was imminent, Rusty pasted a smile on her face and steeled herself.

Right on cue, Reo's gaze found her. He stared...and stared...and stared some more.

"Mr. Sampson," Angie gently prompted when he didn't speak. "I'd like you to meet the woman who handles the parties at our day care, Beatrice Hanson, otherwise known as—"

"Rusty."

Never had any man said her name in just that way, and Rusty struggled to label the tone. Anger? No. Disappointment? Not that, either. Dismay? Maybe...

"You two have met?" Clearly surprised, Angie looked from one to the other of them.

"Yes, as a matter of fact," Rusty answered, when it became evident that Reo wasn't going to.

"You didn't say anything about it." Angie's tone of voice sounded accusing...almost as if she'd picked up on the fact that all was not well and, dedicated personal assistant that she was, intended to find out why.

"I, um, didn't get his name right at the time so didn't realize who he was."

"Oh." Angie waited a moment for Reo to speak, but he still said nothing. "Shall I go reschedule your dinner appointment with Edward Stiles?"

"Yes," Reo said, his gaze never wavering from Rusty.

Angie hesitated for a millisecond before abruptly standing. She handed Reo Sampson his calendar and, with a curious glance at Rusty, left the room.

Rusty could imagine what she thought. She could also imagine what Reo thought. At once the walls seemed to close in. Rusty gripped the arms of her chair and wondered what in the heck to say to this enigmatic man, who continued to stare at her as if under some kind of spell.

"I'm sorry about Friday night." Rusty's explanation fell off her tongue in a rush of words. "Tickets in the trash...Jade couldn't resist...I didn't realize...rented that dress and everything...just wanted to meet some moms...perfect chance...." She sucked in air so she could continue. "Now honestly, could *you* have said no?"

Stunned silence followed Rusty's tangled narrative. Then she saw a smile twitch the corner of Reo's mouth. He leaned back in his chair and crossed his arms over his chest, his steady gaze pinning her to her seat. "Did you just tell me that you crashed that fund-raiser?"

Rusty could've kicked herself. "You didn't know?"

He shook his head. "Is that why you ran out on me? Because you thought I'd found out?"

"Yes. Jade was afraid you'd turn her in to Colleen O'Shaunessy."

"Not likely," Reo murmured with a grimace, adding, "I figured you left because Jade told you my name wasn't really Brad."

"No...though that was a nasty shock." This time it was her gaze nailing him to his chair. "You could've corrected me the first time I called you that."

"Yeah, but I didn't, and that made it impossible to do the next time." He sighed. "Sorry about this job. Angie really thinks you're the one to do it, I suspect she's right."

Rusty's jaw dropped. "You mean you're not going to hire me now?"

"Of course not."

"But why? I'm perfect for this position. Perfect."

"That's immaterial. I don't mix business with pleasure."

"And just who said anything about pleasure?"

He blinked at her. "Why, no one. I just assumed—"

"What? What did you assume?"

"That we'd go out again. Just you and me this time. No aliases, no subplots—"

"No way."

"Excuse me?"

"We're not going out, *Mr.* Sampson. Ever." She added a "so there" nod for emphasis.

He looked stunned. "But why?"

"You're not my type."

"Friday night you kissed me."

"*You* kissed *me*...and that was then, this is now."

"What's different?"

I don't believe this. "You're not Brad, a nice man who works in the mail room for a very large company. You're Reo Sampson, owner of that same company."

"So?"

"So we're obviously a mismatch. I don't do charity balls—not usually, anyway. Nor do I do high finance, fancy cars or gourmet restaurants. You're way out of my league."

"I'm the same man you kissed Friday night," he finally said.

"*You* kissed *me*—" for some reason it was very important that he understood that "—and you *aren't* the same man, therefore it will never happen again. Now how about that job? I really want it."

"You're sure you're over me?"

"*Over you?*" Rusty exclaimed, aghast. "For your information, I was never attracted enough to have to bother." Surreptitiously she crossed her fingers, negating the lie.

"Can we test that statement without your filing a sexual harassment suit?"

"That depends on what kind of test you have in mind."

"Another kiss, only this time you'll know exactly who's on the *receiving* end."

Rusty let that pass. "I really don't think that's a good idea."

"Why? Because you *are* attracted to me?"

"Not in the least. I just...oh, what the hell." She stood and walked around his desk, motioning for him to rise.

Reo sprang from the chair. "Do we need to call Angie in to witness this?"

"Are you insane?"

"Then should I have you sign some kind of waiver? I mean, I wouldn't want you to think of this later and conclude that I took unfair advantage..."

Obviously he was well versed on the issue of sexual harassment. Probably from personal experience. "Though I'm not sure this is a wonderful idea, I have no intentions of suing you later. Now could we please just get this over with?"

"Sure," he answered, reaching out to embrace Rusty.

She stood starch stiff in her determination not to react, yet couldn't wait to taste him again.

"For Pete's sake relax." Reo covered Rusty's mouth with his. His lips moved softly against hers; his tongue teased her teeth for entry. Rusty obliged and was treated to a deeper kiss that resulted in a barrage of the strangest—yet shockingly familiar—sensations.

Her heart began to pound; her stomach, to knot. Goose bumps danced down her arms, yet in other places, private places, she burned. Most distressing of all was her feeling that the room had shifted so that the ceiling, once overhead, now lay in front of her.

Rusty turned her face away from Reo's erotic on-slaught. Gasping for breath, she fumbled for enough wits to accurately assess her surroundings. She realized that the ceiling *was* in front of her, but not because *it* had moved. Oh, no.

Rusty had somehow changed positions, and now lay flat on her back on Reo's big ol' desk with him leaning over—and on—her. While he nuzzled her neck with his lips, she frantically performed a body and clothing check. Hands? Digging into his back. Breasts? Flattened by the weight of his chest. Legs? Shamelessly parted so that his lower body pressed much too close. Feet? One bare. Both up in the air. Clothing? Surely askew since she felt cool breezes in the oddest of places.

"Stop, Reo. Stop!"

Reo instantly tensed and pulled back slightly so that she could see his face. He looked a bit dazed himself, she realized. Dazed and surprised.

Quickly Rusty pushed him away and scrambled off the table. She tugged her skirt down, smoothed her crumpled blouse and jacket, stepped into the shoe that had fallen off.

For at least a minute, they just stared at each other. Rusty wanted nothing more than to run as far and fast as she could, but instead pictured herself pounding the pavement as she searched for a job that would pay as much as this one and result in so respected a reference.

What to do…what to do…?

Impulsively and in desperation, she reached out and straightened Reo's tasteful tie.

"I think we handled that beautifully, don't you?" she asked, as if nothing had just transpired between them. What else was a workingwoman to do?

"'Beautifully.'" He sounded like a robot set on *echo*.

"So I've got the job?" She held her breath.

"'Got the job...'" Abruptly he turned away from Rusty and shifted his gaze to his desk. Haphazardly he began to straighten it. "This is all contingent on the Moreaus of course. We're supposed to meet them at Sartoni's at eight tonight so they can look you over."

Finally he raised his gaze to hers again. She could see he'd regained control of himself. In fact, except for the fact that his glasses were askew and he had a smear of her lipstick on his cheek, he looked like every other wealthy businessman in the city—shrewd and predatory. Rusty retrieved the ever-present tissue from her pocket and handed it to him, pointing to his cheek. Clearly disconcerted, he swiped at the streak of color, then straightened his wire-rimmed specs.

"I'll meet you there," she answered as though she ate at Sartoni's once a week. In truth, Rusty had never set foot in the four-star restaurant. She knew where to find it, however.

"I prefer to pick you up."

"Why?"

"The Moreaus would expect it of me."

"Oh. Well then, Angie has my address."

"Good. I'll see you at seven-thirty."

"Is what I'm wearing now all right?"

Reo's gaze began at the collar of her blouse and moved slowly down to the toes of her navy blue pumps, missing not a detail. He swallowed audibly and looked away, all the while loosening his tie as if he couldn't catch his breath. "Perhaps something, um, softer."

"Softer?"

"You're going to be entertaining little kids. You should look approachable."

"Good point. I'll see you tonight," Rusty said, turning on her heel and striding to the door.

She maintained her composure through her cordial goodbye to Angie and her departure from the office, after which she darted into the nearest ladies' room. There, huddled against a cold marble wall, she shivered in the aftermath of her latest near miss with Reo.

"I must be crazy," she said aloud, well aware of how much smarter it would have been to just find another job. But jobs that paid as well as this one were few and far between. Besides...it was only for a couple of days, and she and the kids she would be entertaining wouldn't see that much of Reo.

Rusty walked over to a sink and turned on the cold water, which she carefully patted on her flushed face to cool it. That done, she repaired her makeup and smoothed her hair. Looking much more like a capable young businesswoman, Rusty opened the restroom door and stepped out into the hall, only to catch a glimpse of Reo, standing outside his office now and talking to another man. At once, she ducked out of sight.

Clearly it was one thing to tell a man she could resist him, yet quite another to actually manage it. Especially an irresistible man like Reo Sampson, whose gruff exterior concealed passion she had only briefly sampled and now wanted desperately to experience to the fullest.

Chapter Four

Rusty pushed the speed limit driving home, knowing it would take most of the afternoon to make her house presentable for Reo. Not that she actually intended to invite the man in when he came knocking on her door. No, indeed. But today's idiotic kiss had proved that accidents happened, and she wanted Reo's future impressions of her to be good ones should he somehow manage to get inside her house.

A glance around the cluttered den told Rusty she hadn't underestimated the huge task ahead. Quickly ditching her business suit, she slipped into jeans and a T-shirt and got to work. Soon the washing machine chugged and the vacuum cleaner roared. Coughing from the dust always stirred up during cleaning, Rusty felt the stare of Bandit, who watched her frantic efforts from his bed in the corner of the room.

"So what are you gawking at?" Rusty grumbled to the curious canine. "I admit we've let the place go a little longer than usual this time, but you've surely seen me clean house before.'' Or maybe not, she admitted a heartbeat later. He was just a pup, after all, and she and Jade did put off domestic chores....

Both women worked hard weekdays and so played hard on the weekends. Their ideas of "play" differed, of course—by Friday night Jade craved a party while Rusty sought anything but. The end result was the same, of course. Housework remained last on their respective lists of to-do's.

"What's all this? Are your parents coming over to-night?''

Rusty jumped at the sound of Jade's question, since she hadn't heard her housemate arrive home. Tossing a freshly fluffed accent pillow on the couch, she turned to answer. "No, my parents are not coming over tonight.''

Jade paled. "Oh, God...are *mine?*''

"Nope.''

"Then who?'' Jade demanded, turning slowly to in-spect the room, now neat as a pin. "The president?''

"Bingo!''

"Oh, yeah, right. And is he bringing the first lady with him?''

"Not that president, doofus. The president of Samp-son Enterprises. Or should I say the CEO?'' Rusty gave Jade a thumbs-up and a grin. "Sorry I forgot to phone and let you know I got the job in spite of everything.''

Jade seemed not to hear the apology or the good news. "Reo Sampson's really coming here?'' A frown knitted her brow.

"That's right. We're going to Sartoni's to meet the parents of the kids I'm going to entertain for a few days...if I pass inspection, that is. They do have the final say.''

"And what time is the famous Mr. S coming by for you?"

"Seven-thirty."

"You do realize it's six forty-five..."

"What!"

Jade nodded. "There was a wreck on the highway. I sat in traffic for almost—Rusty?"

Rusty didn't even glance back as she dashed down the hall and into her bedroom. There she tore off her clothes and headed straight for the shower. Thirty minutes later found her dressed but shoeless in the steamy bathroom, trying to tame naturally curly tresses now damp and resistive to styling.

The doorbell chimed. Bandit barked. Rusty panicked.

"Get the door, Jade!" she yelled, even as she dropped her hairbrush and started for the bedroom. Rusty almost collided with her housemate who hurried not to the front door, but in the opposite direction, to the other bedroom. She held the pup tucked under one arm. "Where are you—"

"To my hidey-hole. You're on your own tonight, kiddo," came the brunette's reply just before she vanished from sight. Rusty heard the bedroom door lock, sure indication that her pal had no intentions of facing Reo Sampson tonight or any other night.

Cursing under her breath, Rusty pivoted sharply and headed for the tiny foyer in her stocking feet. Just as the bell chimed again, she reached the front door and yanked it open wide.

"You're early," she blurted to Reo Sampson, who answered her less-than-charming greeting with a guilty-as-charged shrug. Rusty noted that he kept his hands behind his back as if hiding something.

"One of my character flaws, I'm afraid," he said,

adding, "But I'm pretty sure I'm right on time tonight."
Reo took his hand from behind his back and held out
the strappy black shoes she'd worn to the charity ball
and since forgotten. He gazed pointedly at her feet.

"Thank you," Rusty murmured, highly flustered by
the sudden appearance of the shoes, which evoked uncomfortable memories and reminded her just how vul-
nerable she was when around Reo. She reached through
the door for them. "Actually, these might be a bit much
tonight, but if you'll give me half a minute, I have a
pair more appropriate." Rusty turned toward the bedroom, only to remember her manners and turn reluctantly back around to her guest, who still stood on the
porch. "Would you like to wait inside?"

"Thanks," Reo murmured, stepping right into the
foyer.

Accepting the inevitable with a flustered sigh, Rusty
walked to her bedroom once again. There she stepped
into low-heeled leather shoes dyed a shade of green that
just matched her fitted rayon dress. Rusty allowed herself one quick look in the mirror and an adjustment to
her wide belt before heading once more to the foyer. For
some reason, the sooner she got Reo back out the door,
the safer she'd feel.

But her date was now nowhere in sight.

"Reo?" Rusty called, heading quickly through the
closest door, which led to the den. There she found him
standing by Bandit's bed.

"I thought I heard a dog bark when I rang the bell,"
he explained, most likely in response to her badly concealed alarm that he'd moved without permission.
"Where is the little mutt?"

"In the bedroom," Rusty answered. "His, um, bite is
as bad as his bark."

"Oh, yeah?" He looked a bit doubtful—probably because Bandit's bark was nothing to fear.

"Actually that's an exaggeration. But he can wreck a pair of stockings in two seconds flat, so Jade is keeping him occupied until I get away."

"Jade's here?" Reo suddenly appeared as alarmed as Rusty's housemate when she learned he was coming over.

Rusty bit back a laugh. "Mmm-hmm. Want to say hi to the two of them?"

Reo glanced at his watch. "Maybe later. I don't want to be late."

So he had time to meet the dog, but not Jade, too. Well, Jade wouldn't mind that, Rusty wryly acknowledged as she motioned Reo to follow her to the door. She picked her purse up off the side table and raised her gaze to Reo, now staring at her dress.

"Is this 'approachable' enough?" Rusty asked, suddenly worried that she'd made a bad choice.

"It's fine. Perfect in fact." Reo cleared his throat rather noisily and locked his gaze with Rusty's. She noted for the first time that he wore no glasses tonight, so assumed he must have contact lenses, too. "Ready?"

"I just have to get my driver's license and my money," she answered as she dug them out of the oversize leather bag.

"But I'm driving *and* picking up the tab."

Rusty shrugged and tucked the items into the deep pocket of her dress. "One of *my* character flaws, I'm afraid. I never go anywhere without the means to get back home."

"Wise woman," Reo commented, heading out the door.

Moments later found them in his mode of transportation—a sleek midnight blue Jaguar with leather everything inside. Rusty was properly impressed and said so. "Gorgeous car."

He started the engine and backed the vehicle down the drive.

"I said...*gorgeous car.*"

Reo gave her a blank stare, then blurted, "Oh, uh, thanks." Shifting gears, he put the car in motion once again, then shook his head and sighed softly. "Sorry I'm so distracted. This dinner is very important to me. I've tried to recruit the Moreaus for years. This is as close as I've ever come."

"Maybe you should clue me in on progress so far."

Reo nodded. "Good idea. Kay Moreau, as you already know, is a very talented designer of children's clothing. Her husband, Jeffrey, owns a garment manufacturing company."

"If she designs the clothes and he makes them, why do they need you?" Rusty asked and almost instantly regretted the question.

But Reo never missed a beat. "To market what they've made...to advertise, to distribute. That's what Sampson Enterprises is all about."

"I didn't realize—"

"Yeah, well, this account would be a major coup, let me tell you."

"I'm sure everything will go fine."

"Hopefully." He ran a finger inside the neck of his shirt as if it choked him. "I understand that Jeffrey Moreau is very progressive in his ideas of education and discipline. You might want to keep that in mind should the conversation turn to that sort of thing."

"OK."

"And Kay Moreau is pro women's rights, especially

where equal opportunity in sports is concerned. I understand she's trying to start up a girls' football league in their hometown.''

"I'll keep that in mind."

"Kay and Jeffrey are obviously very big on family—the reason their twin daughters accompany them everywhere. I've met the girls just once, so don't know much beyond the fact that they're five years old. I suppose we'd be smart to plan what you'll talk to them about.''

Rusty almost laughed at his naiveté. "Actually, I've found that where kids are concerned, it's pretty pointless to plan at all. Why don't I just roll with the punches, as usual?''

His eyes widened in alarm. "You're kidding me, right?''

"Wrong. I call a good list of options the best game plan of all."

"But Rusty—"

"Did you or did you not just call me a 'wise woman'?''

Reo hesitated. "I did."

"Well, you were right…at least about entertaining children. Relax, Mr. Sampson. I know what I'm doing, and I do it well. I can handle these kids. You focus on the parents…OK?''

"OK," he agreed with visible reluctance.

Barely ten minutes into his succulent steak, Reo realized all his worries had been for nothing. Rusty easily made friends with the Moreau girls, Kayla and Kelsey, surprisingly intelligent five-year-olds with golden blond hair that reached their waists and eyes as blue as Rusty's sapphire ring. Reo noted that the adult Moreaus, both with the same coloring, appeared more relaxed and friendly than he'd ever seen them.

He attributed this phenomenon to Rusty and her knack for making the dinner seem more like a social than business event. How did she do it? he had to wonder, knowing that was a skill he should master himself. Curious about her technique, Reo chewed thoughtfully, watching and listening closely to the conversation in progress at the moment.

"Yes, I have little—make that *younger*—brothers," Rusty was saying to Kelsey, distinguishable from her identical sister by the purple ribbon tied in her hair and the fact that she dipped her French fries in ranch dressing. "And a big sister, too. My brothers are twins…just like you and Kayla. They're both married. Bit has a son and a daughter. Spin has a baby girl."

"Bit?"

"Spin?"

Rusty's eyes twinkled. "My family is big on nicknames, I'm afraid. In fact Bit is a nickname of a nickname! Short for 'Little Bit,' which he was at one time. 'Course he's six foot four now. But the name is good and stuck to him, anyway."

"How did Spin get his nickname?" Reo heard the fascination in the voice of Kayla, the twin who preferred green ribbon in her hair and good ol' ketchup on her fries.

"When he was little he loved to spin around and around real fast until he was so dizzy he'd just fall right over." Rusty illustrated her words with a carrot stick selected from the healthful vegetable platter on which she dined. "Now he can't even ride the Ferris wheel without tossing his cookies."

Reo winced at her choice of words, so inappropriate

for mealtime, but everyone else at the table simply laughed.

"What about your sister?" Kay Moreau asked around a bite of grilled chicken breast. "What's her nickname?"

"Mouse."

Kelsey and Kayla giggled. "Because she has a tail?"

"No, silly," Rusty good-naturedly retorted. "Because she was so little when she was born...just tiny, according to my mother. And she has light brown hair, too, and bright brown eyes."

Reo thought they couldn't be any brighter than Rusty's, which shone emerald green, flecked with gold, thanks to the flickering flames on the candles.

"Will you give me a nickname?" Kayla asked.

"And me?" chimed in Kelsey.

"Well, sure...when I know you better," Rusty answered. "How about I think about it while we're together? On the very last day, I'll tell you what your new names are, and we'll even have a special christening ceremony to make them official." She suddenly tensed and flashed a guilty smile in the direction of the adult Moreaus. "Assuming I'm the one you want entertaining Kelsey and Kayla for the day or two these business negotiations will take."

"You are," Jeffrey told her. "But I think I should warn you that while the negotiation process may not require more than a day, Kay and I have other issues to discuss with Reo that may take longer."

"We'll take as long as you need," Reo assured him. It was actually going to happen. He could feel it in his bones.

"Absolutely," added Rusty. "I have such a fun time

planned for your girls while you're here in town at the hotel.''

Reo caught her teasing look…heard the subtle emphasis she placed on the word *planned*. He knew that the woman had no plan—at least not a formal one. And, while doing business that way was inconceivable to Reo, he suspected he'd do well to follow her lead this once. Besides, his end of things would definitely be more calculated, structured and predictable—conditions vital to any successful business transaction. Other important factors, in Reo's opinion, included size of the meeting room, type of refreshments, even the shape of the conference table.

''Actually, Jeffrey and I want to suggest alternate arrangements,'' Kay said with a glance at her husband that hinted they might be playing this thing by ear.

Reo nearly choked. With his fork still loaded and raised to his lips, he shifted his gaze to the woman.

''We have property on the Gulf that's been in Jeff's family for years and years. It's called Driftwood Bay. We think it might be better for all concerned if we talk business there instead of here in Shreveport. Reo looks as if he could use a short vacation—'' Kay gave him a kind smile ''—and Rusty and the girls can play in the sand and water while the intricacies of our merger are finalized.''

Finalized. Damn, but Reo liked the sound of that. But a meeting on the beach? Lasting for days? Slowly he lowered his fork. His gaze sought Rusty's. ''Any problems with heading to the beach?''

''Isn't that the name of your summer clothing line?'' Rusty asked instead of answering. ''Driftwood Bay?''

Kay nodded, clearly pleased that Rusty knew so

much. "You're familiar with our product?" she asked before taking a sip of her iced tea.

"Are you kidding? I buy for my nieces and nephews all the time." Rusty leaned forward slightly as if about to share a big secret. "You know that precious mint green romper you had out last year? The one with the seashells appliquéd on the front?"

Kay beamed and nodded.

"I bought six of those little outfits before the end of the season—one for every kid in the family and a few friends' kids, too!" Her smile brightened the whole table. "The clothing is so durable. I can't wait to see the beach house that inspired it. It'll be much more fun than any ol' hotel."

"Then it's settled," Reo said. A wave of feel-good vibes suddenly washed over him, threatening to drown him since he was so unskilled at negotiating them. Though normally averse to the saccharin, the sentimental, tonight Reo reveled in it. From all appearances, the Moreaus would soon be part of his business domain. He would tread a little sugar water anytime for such a prize, and if he found himself going down for the third time, well, Rusty with her easy laugh and magic smile would be there to haul him out.

Besides, a beach house could easily be turned into an office these days, thanks to laptop computers, cell phones and fax machines. Why, he'd never be more than a phone line away from his other work.

"I brought along a map to our place." Jeffrey pulled a piece of folded paper out of his pocket and handed it to Reo. "Shall we meet there, say, Tuesday of next week?"

"Tuesday is fine," Reo assured him just as the waiter arrived with their dessert.

* * *

Business was not mentioned again until Reo killed his engine in Rusty's dark drive around ten that night. He turned to her with a smile and stretched his arm along the back of her bucket seat.

"You were great tonight. I give you full credit for our success so far. You had those girls eating out of your hand in ten seconds flat."

Rusty's teeth flashed white in the shadow of night when she smiled back at him. "Why, thank you, sir. You weren't half-bad, yourself. In fact—" she swiveled around so that she almost faced him and absently smoothed his lapels "—you've revealed definite potential for flying by the seat of your pants. I'd never have suspected you had such a flexible streak, but when the Moreaus said *beach,* well, you just volunteered to bring the suntan oil."

"Ah, but *you'd* actually heard of the place *and* bought some of the clothing."

"It's good stuff—affordable, durable, unisex. I'm telling you, you're going to be *so-o-o* glad when the Moreaus are part of Sampson Enterprises."

. *Not half as glad as I am right now that* you *are.*

Reo's silent reply sprang from his soul uncensored and caught him by surprise. Instantly on guard, he tensed—a reaction Rusty apparently noticed. At any rate she dropped her hands from his lapels and retreated several inches.

"It's late. I'd better go in."

"We could drive somewhere for the dessert we passed on at dinner tonight..." Reo heard himself reply and could have bitten off his own tongue. He never ate dessert. There was, however, another treat he craved at the moment...the taste of Rusty's sweet lips.

"Better not," his companion answered, a reprieve if ever Reo were offered one.

He took it. "Angie will be in touch with arrangements for next week."

"Great."

There was an awkward silence, then Reo reached to open his door.

"Oh, don't get out," Rusty quickly said, laying a hand on his arm to halt his effort. "I know the way to my front door blindfolded."

"That's good," Reo murmured dryly, "since your housemate didn't have the courtesy to leave the porch light on for you."

"Actually, the bulb is out and neither one of us can remember to buy a new one."

"I see. Well...good night, Rusty."

"Good night, Reo." That said, she slipped out of the car and into the dark. Reo saw a flash of light when she opened the front door and vanished inside the house. Then the black of night closed in on him again.

Feeling oddly alone and almost lonesome, Reo started the powerful engine and put the car in motion. Thoughts ricocheted in his head as he sped home—thoughts about the night's coincidences and outcomes. Thank God he'd let Rusty talk him into hiring her that morning. She was just what he needed to guide him through finalizing this venture with the Moreaus.

And to think he'd been *that* close to letting her go, but hadn't—no thanks to any business acumen. No...he could only credit dim wits for his brilliance in hiring her. Proof lay in his agreeing that they'd handled their wild kiss "beautifully" when in fact they'd both lost their heads.

Reo knew that Rusty equaled *Distraction* with a cap-

ital *D*. He also knew that maintaining emotional distance
while sharing a roof with her could well prove more of
a challenge than the tricky business of hashing out a
complex contract with the Moreaus.

But he'd do both, by golly. He'd do both.

He had to. Rusty and the Moreaus were on the same
wavelength—a wavelength totally alien to him. Without
her around to temper his differences in personality, there
would be no contract. He'd have to follow her lead. Gut
instinct told him that.

On Friday, Angie Mallett called Rusty with details of
the next week, as promised. Since driving to Driftwood
Bay would take five full hours, Reo had opted for a
commuter flight to New Orleans at ten on the following
Tuesday morning, from where they'd rent a car and drive
a half hour to the southernmost tip of Louisiana, location
of the Moreaus' stretch of beach.

So four days later found Rusty hurrying through the
Shreveport airport to the appropriate gate, suitcase rolling along behind since she'd chosen not to check it. She
found Reo already there and waiting—no big surprise.
Dressed in khaki pants and a navy blue sports coat, he
epitomized male fashion and desirability. Rusty could
not control the tingle of excitement—almost fear—that
danced up her spine.

A whole week with good-looking Reo on a sunny
beach…*man, oh man.*

Thank goodness they'd have four chaperons along,
not to mention important business to conduct. Reo,
though he probably didn't realize it yet, would have to
lighten up if he wanted to do business with the Moreaus.
Rusty was almost afraid to watch the process, even
though she wanted to confirm that there really was a nice

guy hidden beneath the veneer of always-early businessman. If she was this attracted to Reo the stuffy ex-
ecutive, how would she react to Reo the relaxed house-
guest?

Rusty, lost in her thoughts, noted only absently how
Reo paced the waiting area adjacent to their gate. One
double take later, she squelched her amusement at that
display of Reo's angst. He would not appreciate a comment on his behavior, nor any free advice. In fact, the
words *chill out* would probably only start an argument,
and Rusty didn't want to fight with him.

"Hi," she therefore said as she parked her suitcase
by a chair.

"Hi," Reo answered, halting his march long enough
to plop down nearby. "According to the hostess, the
plane will be leaving right on time."

Of course he'd checked. "I never doubted it for a
moment," Rusty answered.

Reo gave her a sharp look, sure indication that some
of her amusement had come through. "A car is waiting
for us in New Orleans so we should be out of the city
and on our way with a minimum of delay."

"Too bad," Rusty murmured. "Because a delay in
the Big Easy sounds wonderful right now."

"You like New Orleans, then?"

"Love it. What about you?"

Reo shrugged. "It's OK."

"Only OK?" Rusty envisioned the noisy fun that was
Louisiana's most colorful locale.

"Most of my trips there have been business trips, and
I do try to stay focused—"

Oh, dear. "Reo, we need to talk."

"We do?"

"Yes, we do." Though she'd never intended to do

it—had actually vowed not to—Rusty sucked in a fortifying breath and plunged right in. "If you don't relax, you're going to blow this whole deal with the Moreaus."

"Don't be ridiculous. I—" Abruptly he halted. His gaze narrowed as if he'd suddenly thought of or remembered something. "Er, explain what you mean by *relax*."

Rusty did. "I mean quit watching the clock. Quit trying to plan every little detail. Lose the coat and tie."

Reo seemed to weigh her words as if they were gold. "You're right, I expect. Damn." He sat back in the chair, his expression thoughtful. "You remember that night at the charity ball when you commented that most of the guests there weren't normal?"

Rusty nodded.

"Though I don't totally agree, I will admit that *normal* comes in several shades, and my *normal* does not necessarily match *yours* or, unfortunately, the Moreaus'."

Rusty nodded again. "Your point?"

"My point is that I recognize your words have merit, and I'm willing to follow your lead this week…to a certain extent, anyway."

"I don't think you'll be sorry," Rusty said, reaching out to loosen his stylish tie. She had it off him in a flash and next reached for the jacket. Obligingly, he shrugged out of it, then stood and made short work of neatly tucking both into his carry-on bag.

"Better?" he asked, when he'd sat next to her again.

"Much," Rusty told him.

"What next?"

"A brushup on casual living?"

Reo hesitated, then gave in and sat back down by

Rusty. "Bombs away," he murmured somewhat glumly, settling into the chair.

Rusty didn't waste a second before she began a discourse that began with her impressions of the Moreaus' easygoing lifestyle and ended with her conclusions about their priorities, as well as her opinion that he needed to slow his pace to match theirs.

Her eyes flashed with sincerity and enthusiasm. Her hands waved in the air, bringing her words to life. Her lips...her bright red lips...pursed, stretched into a smile, parted in a laugh. Transfixed, Reo watched and listened, his thoughts not on Rusty's message, but on how very nice it would be to take her in his arms and kiss her...hard...on those soft full lips.

"Why, I'll bet Kay works at their kitchen table at home instead of any office. I mean, they're just that way, which means you've got to meet the challenge...lighten up...go with the *mmmph!*"

Only when Rusty wedged her hands between their bodies and pushed Reo back, did he realize he'd actually followed through on his wild fantasy and kissed the woman...right on the mouth in a public airport, for God's sake, with who-knew-who watching.

Well, hell.

Rusty, eyes round with shock, trembling fingers pressed to her undoubtedly bruised mouth, could only stare in disbelief.

"What was that?" she demanded, voice shaking.

"Reo Sampson meeting the challenge?" Reo quipped, trying to salvage his pride, trying to somehow justify what made no sense at all and never would.

Rusty blinked in surprise. Cheeks stained as scarlet as her lips, she stared at Reo for a second without speaking, then rose abruptly to her feet and headed into the nearby ladies' room. Reo almost didn't hear the soft "Excuse me," she tossed back as if an afterthought.

He immediately glanced around, taking note of fellow travelers. No one seemed to have noticed what had transpired. Did he and Rusty look that natural together, then? Like two lovers on holiday, perhaps, or even honeymooners?

Fat chance, Reo decided, but he still stole a moment to try on the role of beau for size. It didn't fit, of course. Two seconds of fantasy told him that. Not only did she have this thing about his money, she was just too different from the women he usually preferred, which meant a relationship with her could only result in high adventure, constant challenge.

Reo hated challenge—at least the romantic kind. Business challenge was another matter altogether and actually quite stimulating since he and any opponent would be willing participants in the contest and well prepared for it.

At that moment Reo's employee returned—color closer to normal, hands now steadier.

"Sorry about that," Reo said the moment she sat next to him again. "I've never attacked before."

"Oh, no?"

He noticed she kept a safe distance away and felt a pang of remorse. "Absolutely not."

"Hmm." Rusty studied him for a moment, and Reo could almost see the wheels of conjecture turning inside her head. "You know, this unusual spontaneity of yours could be taken as a sign you've heard what I've been saying and are actually taking it to heart. Talk about lightening up…" She shook her head in disbelief. Her lips, stretching into a hesitant smile, caught his attention again.

Reo's concentration immediately slipped a notch, and he barely found the strength to drag his gaze away from that hypnotizing mouth of hers.

A challenge?

Hell, yeah…and the worst part was not his lack of skill in romantic entanglements. No, indeed. The worst part was the fact that his beautiful challenger didn't even realize she'd tossed down the gauntlet.

Chapter Five

"Oh, Reo, look!" exclaimed Rusty, bouncing like some little kid in the passenger seat of the rented sedan they'd driven to the beach from New Orleans. "It's my dream house!"

Reo shifted his attention from the fascinating woman beside him to the house at which she pointed, still several yards away at the end of a drive that circled it. According to his map, this was the Moreaus' place. Curious, he stared at the gracefully weathered dwelling with its tin roof and mix-and-match architectural style. He took note of a porch that stretched across the front of the two-story building, a patio that stretched across the back, plus a brick barbecue grill, a hewn-stone picnic table and a yard that was more sand than grass. "*This* is your dream house?"

"Oh, absolutely...or at least one just like it. This particular house is taken, I believe." She grinned.

Shaking his head in bemusement, Reo braked the car and killed the engine near the garage. "The place does have a certain charm, but I can't quite figure out the architecture.''

''I expect it's post-hurricane or, more likely, hurricane*s*,'' Rusty informed him, stressing the plural. ''This stretch of beach has probably been the target for more than one.''

''Probably....'' He continued to stare at the house, trying to imagine what appeal such a rambling antique could hold for a woman as modern as Rusty. ''What, exactly, do you like about it?''

She arched an eyebrow in response to his question. ''Why, the shape, for one thing. It's so...all over the place.''

Reo could only agree with that. ''What else?''

''The bay windows, that balcony, there, and the porch swing. Know what I'd do if that swing were mine?''

He shook his head.

''I'd drag my husband outside every time it stormed so we could wrap up together in a blanket and swing. It would be so cozy. Why, I can almost hear the wind...smell the rain...feel his arms so tight around me.'' She sighed dreamily.

Reo, who found her vision quite erotic, swallowed hard. ''Then a spouse is included in your future plans?''

Rusty looked surprised—no, more like shocked—at the question. ''But of course.'' She frowned. ''Isn't one included in yours?''

''Actually, no.''

''Are you serious?''

''As a stock market crash. I don't have time for that kind of commitment. I've got a business to run.''

''Oh.'' She appeared stunned. ''But what about children? Don't you want children?''

''Can't say that I do.''

Rusty stared at him as though he were some kind of alien or something. "I love kids, myself. I'm going to marry a wonderful man and have at least four."

"Four!" Reo nearly choked. "How old are you? Twenty-five, six?"

"Twenty-eight," she told him somewhat defensively. "Why?"

"You're talking about years of childbearing, Rusty...assuming you're intending to space your kids out, that is." This seemed like a good opportunity to find out if she had the perfect man waiting in the wings or at the least a basketful of boyfriends stashed somewhere. "Unless you've already scheduled your Mr. Right for an imminent walk down the aisle, you're going to run out of time."

"Thanks so much for the reality check," Rusty said snappishly, indicating to Reo that there was no Mr. Right in sight. And though he still didn't know whether she had boyfriends or not, her chilly tone made one thing clear: she had a temper.

"I was just trying to—"

"Well, don't. Oh, there are the girls." In a flash Rusty exited the car and ran to meet the twins, whose approach up the beach Reo had not noticed.

He watched their reunion without getting out of the car, noting that Rusty's bad mood seemed to have vanished as quickly as it had appeared. Where did she get her enthusiasm for life? he had to wonder. Surely not from half-baked dreams and goals that had no roots in reality.

Reo had dreams and goals, himself, among them expanding the business, investing wisely, purchasing prime real estate, and solving the family mystery. The first three, which did not involve matters of the heart, could be carved in stone. As for the fourth—the family mystery—it remained to be seen how quickly Stiles, the New Orleans attorney Reo had just hired, could solve what had turned out to be a baffling riddle involving his grandfather and some woman in New Orleans.

"Are you going to sit alone in that car all afternoon?" Rusty's question, spoken through the lowered window, burst into Reo's musings about the skeleton in his Sampson family closet. Looking up, he found her and the twins standing close by the car.

"No," he murmured, getting quickly out of the vehicle. A glance toward the house revealed that Jeffrey and Kay had stepped off the patio and now waved a greeting. Reo nodded to them before releasing the trunk latch and walking back to retrieve their suitcases and the equipment he'd brought along to turn this house into an office. He felt a sudden burst of anticipation and knew why: the first of *his* dreams—expanding the business— would soon be accomplished.

"Let me help you." Jeffrey Moreau stood beside him now and reached for one of the two suitcases stashed in the trunk. Reo got the other one, plus his briefcase. "What's this?" Jeffrey asked, indicating the facsimile machine, typewriter and cellular telephone left in the trunk.

"My portable office," Reo replied.

"Ah, well you don't need those yet." Jeffrey shut the trunk with a thump of finality that left Reo wondering when, if ever, he *would*. Frustration replaced his anticipation—he wanted to get started now, this minute—and it was all he could do to keep his smile as Jeffrey led the way to the house.

Out of the corner of his eye, Reo saw the girls run

back up the beach. The next instant Rusty fell into step beside him.

"Remember what I told you," she whispered as if picking up on his disquiet. He felt a slight tug on the middle back belt loop of his khaki pants.

Reo sucked in a deep breath, then exhaled slowly, deliberately, in an attempt to relax. Clearly she'd been right when she warned that if he wanted the Moreaus at Sampson Enterprises he would have to do business their way.

"That's better," Rusty next said, her voice still low. She then released the belt loop and closed the distance to the porch steps, where Kay waited, all smiles.

"How was the trip?" their hostess asked as she ushered them onto the patio and then indoors.

"Perfect." Rusty, now standing in what appeared to be the great room, looked all around with interest. Reo could see her eyes light up as she perused the hardwood floors, braided rugs, family photographs and functional furniture before her. That telltale glow told him she loved not only the outside of the house, but the inside, as well.

This time Reo actually sympathized. The room definitely had a warm and earthy feel about it. In fact, he could easily imagine himself stretched out on the oversize corduroy couch near a roaring fire, cuddled up with...

Reo blinked in surprise at the Technicolor vision in his head—a vision involving a very familiar redhead and very few clothes. He caught his breath. Rusty? He still wanted to make love with Rusty, a woman harboring dreams of marriage and procreation *times four?*

Apparently, and that in spite of the fact that his plans by no means matched hers. Had she slipped him one of those love potions good witches mixed? He had to wonder.

"Your house is just incredible," Rusty was saying when a rattled Reo tuned in again. "I love the shape of it, the color of it, everything."

Kay laughed and exchanged a look with her husband. "I'm so glad to hear you say that. The house's history is a bit shady."

"Oh, yeah?" Clearly Rusty's curiosity had been piqued.

"Yeah," Kay admitted. "I think I told you it has been in Jeffrey's family for years and years…?" Kay's gaze shifted from Rusty to Reo and then back to Rusty, who nodded confirmation. "Well, during that time this place has been everything from a pirate's hideaway to a brothel."

Rusty's eyes widened. "Did you say a brothel?"

Kay nodded. "I'm afraid so."

"Wow!" Rusty looked all around, clearly awed. "I knew this house was magic the minute I saw it. Didn't you, Reo?"

"Uh, sure," he murmured, a lie. He'd known it was trouble, and now he knew why. No wonder he fantasized about fun and games on the couch instead of signing contracts. The spirits of some lusty ladies haunted these halls and now, it seemed, his thoughts.

"I can't tell you how many times Jeff, the kids and I have escaped to Driftwood Bay when life got too crazy. Things invariably start looking better the minute we arrive—thanks to the change in point of view, I guess— and we always reprioritize, which turns big problems into little ones."

"I love your house." Reo heard a decidedly wistful

note in Rusty's voice. "It's absolutely the most wonderful one in the world."

"Where do you live?" asked Jeffrey of Rusty.

"In a very ordinary dwelling in a Shreveport suburb. At the moment with a friend."

"A man-type friend?"

"Jeffrey Moreau!" scolded Kay. "That's none of your business."

"I was just wondering," her husband mumbled, looking a little sheepish.

Rusty laughed and put him at ease. "Actually, my friend is a woman I've known since grade school. Sharing the rent works for us now, but I plan to own a place of my own someday—a place with as many nooks and crannies as this one."

Kay beamed. "We also have a few secret doors, plus an attic just full of stuff."

"I'm in heaven," Rusty said with a heartfelt sigh that made everyone—even Reo—laugh. Clearly she had the Moreaus in her pocket. Hell, she had Reo there, too.

"I suspected you were a romantic," Kay said with a chuckle.

Reo guessed it took one to know one. Kay Moreau, with her upswept blond tresses and colorful peasant dress, looked as much the heroine of some romantic chic flick as did Rusty, who today wore her hair in a single French braid tied with a bow that exactly matched her flowing cotton sundress.

"Now if you two will follow me upstairs, I'll show you to your rooms." Kay led the way up a staircase that creaked with every step, then down a long hall. "The last time we remodeled, we assigned each room a theme, based on Moreau family history. Reo, I'm putting you in here." She indicated a door on their left. "I call this room the Captain's Room. Supposedly, our pirate slept in there when he was beached." She pointed a little farther down the hall. "Rusty, you'll be next door."

"What do you call my room?"

Kay smiled. "The Red Room. When you get in there, you'll see why. That third door leads to the bathroom. The rest of us sleep downstairs." She gave them a gracious smile and touched Reo's arm. "Now isn't this more fun than a stuffy hotel?"

"Yes, indeed," he agreed, perhaps a shade too heartily. In truth, he found the legends and themes highly disconcerting; the cluttered decor, distracting; Rusty's proximity, damned disturbing.

If Kay suspected his insincerity, she didn't comment on it, instead leaving them to settle in while she went to the kitchen to prepare a snack to "tide everyone over" until dinnertime. Rusty darted right into her room, suitcase in tow, and while Reo examined his own sleeping quarters, he listened to her exclamations of delight over the bed, the bay window, the view of the beach, even the lamps, for Pete's sake.

Reo decided the walls must be made of paper before he realized that the separation between the two rooms was not a real wall at all, but a divider of sorts that didn't quite reach the ceiling.

With a sigh, he sat on the built-in bed, testing it for bounce as he took in the nautical furnishings of the room. He felt as if he were below deck on a pirate ship. Shaking his head in bemusement, Reo abruptly left the room and headed next door to Rusty's. He found her on her knees on a window bench, leaning way too far out as she waved and called to Kayla and Kelsey on the beach below.

"Damn, Rusty!" Reo exclaimed, rushing forward to grab her by the ankle.

She ducked back into the room at once. "I'm not going to fall."

"Not *now,* no." He still held on.

"Do you mind?" Rusty asked, shaking her foot.

When Reo released her, she tucked a leg under her and sat on the red velvet window bench.

Red velvet? Belatedly Reo took stock of the room. He saw red and gold paper on the walls; heavy red drapes on the windows and the canopy bed; patterned red rugs on the floors; and red velvet on the benches, chairs and in the bedspread.

"Holy—"

Rusty giggled. "Naughty, isn't it?"

"That's one word for it," Reo muttered, sitting beside her.

Rusty giggled again. "I'm going to sleep like a baby in that." She rose and patted the massive bed.

"Only if I don't snore," Reo retorted, pointing out the gap between partition and ceiling.

Rusty bubbled with laughter. "Great. We can whisper together after lights-out."

"After what?"

"Lights-out." She frowned at what must be his blank expression. "Didn't you ever go to camp when you were a kid?"

"No."

"Well, *lights-out* is when the camp counselor turns out the lights each night so everyone will go to sleep. We weren't supposed to talk after that, though we did, of course."

"You went to camp every summer?"

"From the age of five on, and so did my brothers and

my sister. Mom saved for it all year. Then, while we were in the woods learning about nature, she and Dad took a road trip to some place they'd never been.'' She laughed as though suddenly remembering something. ''I believe I was a real pain in the butt to my siblings my first year at camp. As I recall, they didn't even claim me as family. Then in a couple of days I became a human being, and they weren't so mortified.'' Rusty's questioning gaze found his. ''I'm getting a weird vibe, here. Didn't you ever embarrass your brothers and sisters when you were little?''

''I don't have any,'' Reo said.

''None at all?'' She looked horrified.

Reo shook his head.

''Well, no wonder you don't want kids. You don't know what fun they are. Why, I remember when my brothers were lit—'' Rusty broke off at the sound of Jeffrey's voice, calling to his girls. Reo heard the sound in stereo since it floated up the stairs and came in through the open window.

''Our snack must be ready,'' he murmured, heading gratefully to the door. The last thing he needed was a sentimental walk down memory lane with Rusty. Besides, the walls of her wicked bedroom seemed to be closing in, and the resulting intimacy bothered him. Nonetheless he hesitated in the doorway. ''Or should we wait to be called?''

''I say we save our host the trouble,'' Rusty said, rising to slip past him and into the hall. Their bodies brushed ever so slightly—just enough to set Reo on fire for his employee and make him wish he could coax her back to that big scarlet bed.

They would let down the curtains and their hair, making excellent use of the privacy thus created. The springs in that old mattress would sing out a sexy song, one these walls had undoubtedly heard countless times before—

"Is Sampson Enterprises taking care of meals while we're here?"

"Hmm?"

Rusty, who now led the way down the hall, stopped so suddenly that Reo crashed into her. Pivoting sharply, she frowned at him.

"I asked if Sampson Enterprises is paying for the food. I don't want to take advantage of the Moreaus."

"Oh, uh, sure." With effort Reo dragged his thoughts away from her sexy red bed. "Er, actually…what I meant was no. Though Angie did her best to work that out, even to the point of volunteering to send a cook or, at least, groceries, the Moreaus wouldn't hear of it. Apparently Kay loves to entertain, which might be the real reason for the switch in location. I'll admit I'm still baffled about that since a bordello is hardly the best place to conduct business."

"Actually, if this house really was a brothel, business mergers much more interesting than the one you have in mind have already been transacted here lots of times."

"Good point," Reo muttered, even though she'd really be shocked by the kind of merger on his mind at the moment.

Grateful for the sunshine streaming through the bay window and for the cheery yellow color scheme—a sharp contrast to the sensual red upstairs—Reo nodded a greeting to Jeffrey, busy seating his girls at a huge wooden table.

"We're just having cheese dip, salsa and chips," Kay said.

"Doesn't sound very Cajun," Rusty teased.

"That's because the cook is a Texan," Kay replied with a grin, motioning for Rusty and Reo to join the girls and Jeffrey at the table.

Minutes later the crunch of chips obviated the need for conversation as they all sampled the spicy concoction, then cooled their mouths with lemonade. Rusty's compliment to the chef led to a discussion on food, specifically Tex-Mex, and before Reo knew it, a solid hour had slipped by. He marveled that he hadn't thought of contracts, time wasted or his office even once in that sixty minutes.

Good, he thought. Or maybe not so good...if he was so damned drunk on atmosphere that he couldn't concentrate on business.

"Why don't you girls show Rusty around the house, then take her to the beach," Jeffrey suggested. "Your mom and I want to talk to Reo for a bit, then we'll barbecue chickens, just like I promised."

"OK," Kelsey said, slipping out of her seat. Kayla followed suit, as did Rusty.

"Can we go to my room first?" Rusty asked the girls. "I'd like to change into something more comfortable."

With a nod Kayla darted from the kitchen. Taking Rusty's hand, Kelsey led her through the door and into the hall. Reo, shaken by Rusty's careless "change into something more comfortable" comment, gave himself a mental kick in the butt, drew in a fortifying breath and turned his full attention to Jeffrey.

"Shall I get the contract I've had drawn up?"

Jeffrey nodded. "We may as well get that out of the way first. Then Kay and I want to brainstorm with you on a new project. Something totally different from anything we've ever done."

As curious as he was ready to get down to business,

Reo nodded and headed straight upstairs to get his briefcase. While in his room, he steadfastly ignored the tantalizing girl talk coming from the boudoir next door—
or, rather, *little*-girl talk in the form of questions fired at
Rusty in rapid succession: "...always wear bikini panties?" "...have a boyfriend?" "...in love with Reo?"

The last question caught Reo's attention, of course,
and in spite of himself, he paused and tuned in to Rusty's
reply.

"Reo is my boss, Kayla, not my boyfriend."

"But he's so-o-o handsome." That singsong comment
made Reo grin.

"Yes, he is. But he's still my boss, which means he
can't be my boyfriend."

"What if he wasn't your boss? Could you love him
then?"

Yeah, could you? Reo silently echoed.

"That depends," Rusty answered.

"On what?" Still frozen to the spot, Reo mouthed the
predictable question even as one of the twins—he didn't
know which—uttered it.

"On whether or not he could love me—"

I could, darlin'. Oh yeah, I could.

"—in the very special way I want to be loved."

Or maybe not.

"What special way is that?" The voices were right
outside Reo's door now, in the hall, and he took a quick
step back so the females would not catch him eaves-
dropping.

"Oh, let's just call it a happily-ever-after, fairy-tale
kind of way. I want to get married just like your mama
and daddy did, except I want to have four children. I
think Reo Sampson is too busy for a wife, not to mention
that many kids."

"I know someone who has time to get married and have kids."

"Really? Who?" Their voices had begun to fade with their descent down the stairs. Reo had to strain to hear the rest.

"My uncle Jacques."

"And just how do I meet this marvelous man?"

Reo heard no more.

Well, hell, he thought as he snatched out the contract prepared by the Sampson lawyers yesterday. Highly miffed with those twins for asking Rusty so many stupid questions—not to mention Rusty for her equally stupid answers—Reo hurried back to the kitchen table, which was now spotless, thanks to Kay's efforts.

Steadfastly closing his mind to everything not connected to this imminent, critical business venture, he sat across from Kay and Jeffrey, gave them each a copy of the contract and began a line-by-line explanation.

"So Uncle Jacques is your father's brother?" Rusty and the girls now walked along the beach, picking up shells and placing the prettiest in a plastic bucket. The three o'clock sun felt good on Rusty's bare arms, and she was glad she'd chosen pants instead of shorts, which wouldn't have been enough for the low-sixties temperatures.

"Uh-huh," Kayla said. "And I know he likes weddings 'cause he's been in three."

"As best man?"

Kelsey shook her head. "As the husband."

"You mean your uncle Jacques has been married three times?"

"Uh-huh." Neither girl seemed perturbed by the number.

"Hmm. Well, that's two too many for me," Rusty told them, mentally drawing a line through the name *Jacques Moreau* on her list of possibles.

Not that Rusty normally maintained such a list. She didn't. Nor did she usually judge men based on their feelings about marriage. Today, however, thanks to Reo's less-than-tactful comments about time running out, she seemed to be doing both.

"Let's race," Rusty impulsively suggested, hoping a jog up the beach would clear her head. With squeals of enthusiasm, the girls began to run, and soon the three of them loped along together holding hands and laughing. Rusty couldn't remember when she'd felt so carefree, and she cherished the feeling for the next three hours while she and the twins played in the sand near the water.

During that time, she took note of the differences in the personalities of her charges. Kayla, she realized, was a tomboy—eager for physical challenge, full of outrageous ideas, quick to think up and then tire of any activity. Kelsey, on the other hand, held back when it came to trying something new or challenging and didn't abandon anything until she'd completed it.

The sun had begun to sink on the horizon before Kay called Rusty and the girls back to the house. There they found Jeffrey lighting a fire, and Reo standing at the picnic table wrapping baking potatoes in aluminum foil. Kay was in the kitchen, and Rusty went inside to help in any way she could, while the twins offered their services to their dad, now fanning flames.

Kay, busy with the salad, instructed Rusty on how to shuck the corn and season it. Once that was done, Rusty joined Reo outside at the picnic table, where she borrowed the aluminum foil and tore off enough sheets to individually wrap the buttered and salted ears of corn.

"How's it going?" Rusty whispered to Reo when she was sure Jeffrey wasn't listening. He stood across the table from her.

"So far, so good. What about you?"

"I've had a very enlightening afternoon, actually."

"I'm surprised you didn't ask to borrow my cell phone," Reo muttered, giving her a sharp look.

Rusty frowned. "Whatever for?"

"To call Uncle Whatsisname...the guy who likes weddings?"

So he'd eavesdropped. Interesting. "The girls didn't know his number."

"You asked them for it?"

"Of course not," she told him, impishly adding, "Though I was tempted...until I learned he likes weddings a little too well." She leaned across the table and lowered her voice. "I have it on good authority he's been divorced three times."

Reo's gaze locked with hers. It was clear to her that he didn't know whether she was teasing him or not.

Though Rusty tried to keep a straight face, she couldn't and so wound up bubbling with laughter, a dead giveaway that brought a flush to Reo's face. Shaking his head in disgust, he turned his back on her and carried the wrapped potatoes to Jeffrey. Rusty made the most of the opportunity to study him undetected.

In these surroundings and without his stuffy coat and tie, he looked like any middle-class American male on vacation...in other words a man Rusty could safely love. And though she knew he really wasn't, she found it incredibly easy to indulge in a fantasy that she and Reo were married guests and that they would later slip up-

stairs and make love to the sound of the waves crashing
against the shore.

At that moment Reo turned and caught Rusty staring.
He gave her a sheepish grin that turned her knees to
Jell-O and mind to mush. Shocked by the intensity of
her instantaneous physical response to him, Rusty fell,
more than sat, on the stone bench and struggled to focus
on the task at hand.

Was it the impact of a full coral moon, rising in the
eastern sky, that mysteriously exaggerated every feeling
of desire she'd ever felt for Reo? Was it the house, rich
in color, texture and history that made her suddenly
scheme ways to lure him upstairs alone to that red, red
room?

Or was it the man, himself—looking handsome as any
fairy-tale prince and close enough to kiss?

Probably all three, Rusty decided, practically tossing
the wrapped corn at Jeffrey in her haste to escape indoors. Once there, she stayed there, only occasionally
giving in to temptation and peeking out the window to
the patio, now lit with patio torches. Her gaze unerringly
found Reo each time, and she noted how well he got
along with Jeffrey and his daughters.

Things were going well…at least businesswise. Unfortunately Rusty's heart was definitely the worse for
wear. What was it about this man, she wondered, that
made her thoughts turn to weddings and honeymoons?
She knew next to nothing about him, for heaven's sake,
and what she did know was more than enough to send
her packing.

"Rusty?"

The loud whisper barely penetrated the partition between the upstairs bedrooms, much less Rusty's sleep, so it wasn't hard to convince herself that she dreamed.

"Hey...Rusty!"

No dream that, but Reo calling out to her from next door. Against her will, Rusty pried open her eyes and reached for her bedside clock: 2:00 a.m. Good grief. "What do you want?"

"An antacid. Do you have any?"

"Not handy. Go ask Kay for one," Rusty muttered, burrowing into the mattress, slipping off to sleep again.

"Now what kind of guest would ask the cook for an antacid?"

The same kind who would wake up a totally-exhausted baby-sitter? "OK. OK. I'll look in my bag." With a groan Rusty threw back the sheet and crawled out of the bed. She felt drugged, almost dizzy with sleep, and instantly caught her foot on a chair leg. "Damn!"

"Are you all right?"

"No, I am not all right. I just broke my little toe on this stupid—are you laughing?"

"Not me," he answered, his voice suspiciously thick.

Rusty saw red—and not because of her room assignment. Muttering another curse, she snatched up her toiletries bag and began to riffle through it for some antacid tablets to ease Reo's indigestion. "Aha!"

"You found some?"

"Yes. Want me to toss them over the partition?" Not for nothing had she played softball in high school.

"Better meet me in the hall."

With a sigh of impatience, Rusty headed for the door. She opened it to find Reo already standing there in the shadows, bare-chested and barefoot. As for what he wore between those two bare points, she couldn't say, since she immediately glued her gaze to his chin and kept it there, well above the sculptured pecs and washboard abs she'd glimpsed.

"Take two and call me in the morning."

"Very funny," Reo said, snatching the package and popping two tablets into his palm. He swallowed them in one gulp without water and then handed the rest back to Rusty. "How's the bed?"

"Wonderful. How's yours?"

"It's more a berth than a bed, actually. My room looks like the captain's quarters on a sailing ship."

"Really?" Curiosity propelled Rusty right through the hall and into Reo's bedroom, bathed in moonlight and looking for all the world like the set of a swashbuckling pirate movie. "Oh, Reo, this is so realistic."

"Yes, all that's missing is the waves...thank God. I'm nauseated enough."

"It was that last piece of chicken, you know."

"Don't remind me," Reo groaned, sitting down on the bed, then falling back, his hand on his belly.

In spite of herself, Rusty took note of the stylish boxer shorts he wore and his legs, long and muscular. Her heart began that irritating flutter that she'd felt on the patio earlier. "I'm going back to bed now."

"I'm dying, and you're leaving. What kind of employee deserts her boss in his time of need?"

"A smart one," Rusty whispered, pivoting to exit. She managed one step before Reo sprang up and caught her wrist in an iron grip.

"What did you say?"

Rusty sighed. "I said 'a smart one.'"

"And what's that supposed to mean?"

"It means that this employee knows her limits, and the sight of the boss in nothing but silk boxers and glasses is definitely her limit."

Reo abruptly released her. "You think it's any easier for me, seeing you in that?"

"It certainly should be," Rusty muttered, knowing the oversize New Orleans Saints T-shirt that covered her from neck to knees was anything but sexy.

"Well, it's not. In fact, I don't think I've ever seen you look so good." His gaze moved over her, gentle as a lover's caress and twice as stimulating as it lingered first here and then there.

Rusty, who could barely breathe, struggled to lighten the moment. "You're sick. I'm outta here." She whirled toward the door.

Reo caught her by the arm. "Actually, I'm feeling much better now. In fact, I think you cured me."

"Sure I did," Rusty returned dryly, shaking off his touch and heading resolutely for the door. "Good night, Cap'n Sampson."

"Good night, m'lady."

M'lady? His cryptic words stopped her cold. Slowly she turned, her confusion undoubtedly on her face.

"If I'm the captain," Reo explained, "then you must be the beautiful captive."

"B-beautiful captive?" Forgetting Reo's aching stomach just as quickly as he apparently had, Rusty clutched the doorjamb to keep from falling in a heap of unrequited passion at his bare feet.

"Damned beautiful captive…you know, the daughter of the wealthy nobleman—"

"My father isn't wealthy."

"The daughter of a *peasant,* kidnapped and held on board for the captain's pleasure." He stepped close. Too close.

Rusty pressed her back to the wall. "I've seen this movie."

"Then you remember what happens," Reo said, placing his hands on the wall behind Rusty, holding her prisoner.

"Actually—" Rusty splayed her fingers on his bare chest as though to push him away, although she didn't "—I seem to have forgotten."

"Why, the beautiful captive falls for the sex-crazed captain, of course," Reo replied and then covered her waiting mouth with his.

Chapter Six

And what a kiss it was—the fiery result of a whole day of "look, but don't touch."

Well, Rusty touched now, moving her lips over Reo's lips even as she moved her hands over his chest and arms. He felt so damn good—so masculine, so sexy and strong. Rusty gently tugged Reo's glasses off his face and set them on a nearby table out of harm's way, then slipped her hands behind his neck and laced her fingers, a maneuver that couldn't be accomplished properly until she raised her bare heels from the floor for extra height.

Reo responded by wrapping his arms around Rusty and holding her tightly against the wall of his body while he kissed her thoroughly. She felt the hammering of his heart, the heat of his arousal. Though warning bells should have sounded, they didn't. This was the movies, after all. The action never stopped until the director yelled, "Cut!" And the director never yelled "Cut!" when a scene sizzled like this one.

Rusty trailed her mouth over Reo's chin, rough with

whiskers. Half-drugged by the scent of his cologne, she sniffed and nuzzled and then tasted, stopping only when Reo abruptly scooped her up in his arms and carried her to his bed. The mattress dipped with his weight when he stretched out beside her a second later.

"What are you doing?" Rusty asked even as she let him grasp the hem of her sleep shirt in his hands and pull it clean over her head.

"Getting closer," he answered, adding a heart-stopping kiss that involved her bare breasts, his tongue and a lot of heavy breathing.

"Clo-ser?" she said, panting.

"Much closer," Reo promised, getting rid of her bikini panties in one smooth move, thanks to her cooperation. He then rolled over so that his weight pressed Rusty into the mattress. His hands were everywhere, just as hers were—touching, teasing, tantalizing. She relished the sensation of cool silk on heated flesh, and was only vaguely grateful for the boxers that were all that prevented consummation.

Consummation? Didn't that lead to…babies? And before one had babies, shouldn't one marry?

That *was* the master plan.

So why was she lying naked on the bed of a man—a very rich man—who wasn't interested in anything more long term than stock and bonds.

Rusty didn't have a clue, so panicked. "Stop, Reo. Stop."

He froze—undoubtedly in response to the horror in her voice. Or was it because he'd heard these same words before and knew what came next? "What is it?"

"I-I can't do this."

"Why not?" His face was so close to hers that his features looked fuzzy.

"I just can't."

Long seconds passed during which Rusty heard every shaky breath Reo drew. Embarrassed to have been the cause of what must surely be the worst case of sexual frustration in the history of *this* house, Rusty lay still as could be, eyes now squeezed tightly shut. Finally he rolled off her and onto his back. The mattress shifted and dipped as he got off the bed. Only when she heard the sounds of a suitcase being opened, did Rusty risk a peak at Reo.

He was nothing more than a silhouette against the wall of moonlit windows—a silhouette that slipped on a short robe, then made his way out of the room. At once Rusty groped around for her T-shirt and panties, both of which she finally located. She dressed quickly and headed for the door, only to stop and think twice, something she wished she'd done much, much sooner.

They had to talk—she and Reo. What happened tonight could not be ignored. Never mind that she was still on fire for him, and he, for her. They could control their passions long enough to plot tomorrow. Surely, surely they could.

On hearing the floor creak outside Reo's door, Rusty froze and then turned to face where he would enter the room. Instead of doing that, he walked on to her door.

"Rusty?"

When Rusty heard his soft knock, his whisper, she let out her pent-up breath in a hiss of relief. So he wanted to talk, too. Good. No, excellent. "I'm still in here."

Creak. Creak. In seconds he stood in the doorway, nothing more than an uncertain shadow in a room aglow with moonlight.

"We need to talk," he told her.

"That's why I waited," she answered.

Reo crossed over to the bed and removed the blanket from it. "Wrap up in this," he said, handing it to Rusty.

Though plenty warm—still hot, really—she did as he requested. He then motioned for her to sit in one of the leather chairs near the window. While she settled in, he sat in the other, but only after dragging it several feet farther away. To her left lay the bank of windows and Reo; to her right, the rest of the room. Shadow obscured his expression.

"Want to tell me what that was all about?" he softly asked.

"I'm not sure I know."

"Is this…are you…what I mean is—"

"Have I done this before?"

She could barely see his confirming nod.

"The answer is yes," Rusty admitted with candor. "But not since I figured out what I want out of life, and never with a man like you."

"And what kind of man is that?" He sounded offended.

"One who's all wrong for me. I could fall for you, Reo Sampson. I could fall for you even though we don't have a single dream in common. That's very, very dangerous for me."

"For both of us," he said.

"You mean—" She couldn't begin to imagine he felt the same. "Are you saying?…"

"That I could fall for you, too?" He sighed. "Hell, yeah. That's what I'm saying." The silence grew heavy before he spoke again. "What a screwed-up mess. And this last business—" he motioned toward the bed "—well, it was all my fault. I take full responsibility."

"How can you say that?" Rusty asked, irritated that

he would assume all blame, a ridiculously boss-ly thing to do. "I was a willing—no, eager—participant."

"Maybe so, but this would never have happened if—"

"Either of us had been thinking?" she interjected sharply.

Reo hesitated for just a second before agreeing. "Right."

"Well, it did happen, and what I want to know is how we're going to handle ourselves tomorrow."

"Exactly as we did before tonight, of course," Reo answered.

"Would that be when I offered to buy you a beer that first time we met *or* when we kissed at the charity ball, or your office, or the airport?" She could not keep the sarcasm from her tone, and with good reason. They'd misbehaved from the moment they met.

Reo's soft groan was his only reply—sure sign he'd just realized it, too. "This contract with the Moreaus is very important to me."

"And my dreams, believe it or not, are very important to me."

"Then you agree it would be better for all concerned if we keep our relationship purely professional from now on."

"I've always agreed with that." *For all the good it did.*

"That's great, because I have, too."

"Then what is the problem?"

"I'm damned if I know. It's almost as if we've both drunk a love potion or something." Reo suddenly leaned forward, bringing his face into the light. Rusty saw his frown. "You were kidding that day at the elevator when you said all that stuff about mixing potions, weren't you?''

''Of course I was.''

''I knew that.'' He sat back and said nothing for long moments. ''Whatever the reason for this crazy attraction we have for each other, we're just going to have to cope. Do you agree?''

''I agree.''

''Good. Now you go to your room. I'll stay here in mine. And tomorrow we'll start right where we left off at dinner.''

At dinner? When she wanted *him* for dessert? Rusty's spirits sank to her bare toes. Suddenly irritated with herself and with Reo, who was only trying to do the right thing and didn't deserve her wrath, Rusty got to her feet. ''We're both adults. We should be able to do that.''

''Excellent.'' He stood, too. ''Good night, Rusty.''

''I think that should be good *morning,*'' she retorted with not a little sarcasm, handing him his blanket and exiting the room.

Reo slept maybe five minutes the rest of Tuesday night, thanks to his hyperactive hormones and a worsened bellyache. Judging from the squeaks and shuffling next door, Rusty wrestled her blankets, too.

In his mind he replayed their lovemaking and felt again the softness of her skin, the fullness of her curves. The memory of her sweet, sweet kisses would haunt him for a long time, he realized, maybe even forever. That made things tough, but not unbearable. He was, after all, a man used to disappointment. He knew how to put it behind him, how to distract himself by setting a new goal. Never mind that Rusty had never really been a goal at all…at least a logical one. She was like everything, everyone else in his life these days: expendable. He could and would survive without her.

Breakfast with the Moreaus turned out to be a noisy, chaotic affair. Jeffrey, who'd made an early-morning run to the bakery down the road, served sweet rolls and doughnuts of every shape and size, while Kay offered hot chocolate, coffee, fruit juice and milk.

Though not a bit hungry, thanks to the previous night's melodrama, Rusty managed to choke down a Danish. She noted that Reo ate with gusto, sure indication his tummy had survived last night's spicy chicken and the extracurricular activities afterward.

Following breakfast, Rusty and the girls retired to the beach as they had the day before, leaving the adult Moreaus and Reo to conduct business. The sun shone warmer today, and by ten the temperature reached the mid seventies, reason enough to slip into bathing suits and catch some rays.

Kelsey wore a purple bikini; Kayla, a green one. With the radio playing golden oldies—the twins' choice, not Rusty's—the three females stretched out on beach towels at the water's edge and talked away the rest of the morning.

The occasional breeze raised goose bumps on Rusty's flesh, but she didn't mind. With Reo out of sight, it was easy to pretend this was just another baby-sitting job, and her life would go on as it always had once she got back home.

When the girls suggested a picnic at lunch, Rusty readily agreed. Noon found them dining royally on peanut butter and jelly sandwiches, served under the shade of a huge beach umbrella. Dressed now in shorts and shirts, they laughed a lot, and in spite of herself, Rusty began to feel better. Thoughts of what had transpired between her and Reo the night before receded into the darkest corners of her mind, and she deliberately kept them there.

By the time the sun began to sink on the horizon, Rusty actually enjoyed herself again. Even Kay's calling them in to dinner did not dampen her good mood, and the bright smile she pasted on her face stayed in place for most of the meal.

"Will you play Sorry! with us?" Kayla asked Rusty after dinner, referring to a children's board game Rusty had loved as a kid. They all sat in the great room—Reo and Jeffrey on the couch, Kay in a rocker, and the twins and Rusty on giant pillows on the floor.

"Rusty's played with you all day," interjected Kay. "Don't you think she deserves a break?"

"Oh, I don't mind a game or two," Rusty answered. It certainly beat the heck out of sitting around, trying not to look at Reo.

"It's more fun with four players," said Kelsey. She turned to Reo. "Want to play?"

"I don't know how," he answered, words that earned him a look of pity from the twins.

"We'll teach you," volunteered Kelsey.

"It's easy," added Kayla.

"You don't have to," Jeffrey said, when Reo rose to the inevitable.

"A couple of games won't kill me," he answered, moving to help set up the card table already retrieved from a nearby closet by Kayla.

Minutes later found all four seated at the table with the colorful game board in front of them. Rusty, determined to prove that last night didn't matter one bit, played with gusto and studiously avoided Reo's gaze. It wasn't easy. The man sat right across the table with his knees brushing hers every time he squirmed, which was too often.

He lost the first game, but won the next, much to the twins' chagrin. Pronouncing the win "beginner's luck," Reo turned down the offer of a third game, instead heading outside to his car to get his laptop computer. Claiming he needed to "do some catch-up work," he then went upstairs.

Rusty heaved a sigh of relief when he left, but quickly became bored. She faked having a good time until nine-thirty, then excused herself and headed up the stairs to bathe before bed. Once there, she discovered that Reo was already in the bathroom, showering. Rusty waited for him to finish and get back to his bedroom before venturing from hers.

A relaxing bath later, she went back to her room and crawled into her big old bed. Rusty hoped sleep would come quickly, but it eluded her tonight, thanks to the sensual memories that came out of hiding. It didn't help that Reo's light, visible over the top of the partition, stayed on until the wee hours of the morning, or that she could hear every time he sighed. Finally Rusty could stand her solitude no longer.

"Reo?" she called, her voice a loud whisper.

"Are you still awake?" came his immediate reply.

"Yes, and I'm wondering why you are."

"I'm modifying the contract we finally agreed on today."

"So the Moreaus are now part of Sampson Enterprises."

"They will be, when they sign on the dotted line tomorrow."

"Congratulations."

"Thanks."

There was a long silence after that. Assuming Reo had gone back to work, Rusty burrowed into her blankets and tried, once again, to sleep.

"Rusty?"

She smiled. "What?"

"I'm really sorry about last night."

"Because you didn't enjoy it?" she asked—a question blurted from the heart.

"You know better."

"Then why?"

"Because—" He hesitated so long she thought he really had no answer. "Because I was disrespectful of your dreams. I knew what you wanted. I knew I didn't want the same things. Yet I still came on to you."

"And I let you—" she shook her head in disbelief "—even though I still believe you have too much money for the likes of middle-class me. You know what I think, Reo? I think we're both victims—victims of unexplainable sexual chemistry, our enforced proximity, even this wicked, wicked house."

"Maybe."

"There's no *maybe* to it. And I want you to understand that while I do have regrets about the things we did, I have just as many beautiful memories."

"I'll never forget it, either."

"You mean that?"

"I do."

"I'm glad," Rusty responded.

Thursday dawned another beautiful day. Since the temperatures hovered in the seventies again, Kay, Jeffrey and Reo worked at the picnic table on the patio. They could see Rusty and the twins building sand castles, and more than once Reo's gaze and attention drifted that way.

"She's very lovely," commented Kay on one of those occasions.

"And good with kids," added Jeffrey.

Reo noticed the couple staring speculatively at him and flushed guiltily. "Yes to both. I'm lucky to have her as an *employee*."

"I'm surprised she's not married," Kay next said, clearly undaunted by Reo's gentle reminder of Rusty's status in his life. "Or is she one of those modern women not interested in husbands and babies?"

"I believe that both are in her game plan," Reo said.

"Are they in yours?" Kay then asked.

"For heaven's sake, honey...." It was Jeffrey's turn to scold.

"Sorry. It's just that Reo, here, is what used to be known as an A-prime bachelor, and I'm wondering how he's managed to avoid the altar for this long."

"Marriage is not on my agenda," Reo answered. "At least not for a while yet." Now where had that come from? he instantly wondered, since marriage was not on his agenda *at all*.

"Well, I'm glad you haven't totally eliminated it from your future," Kay said, reaching over to pat his hand. "Your work won't keep you warm at night when you're old and gray, you know."

"My work doesn't keep me warm at night now," Reo told her.

Jeffrey laughed at that and tugged a lock of his blushing wife's hair. "I think our guest has just told you he's discovered those modern women you mentioned a minute ago."

"Something like that," Reo lied. In truth, girlfriends

of the sleepover variety had been few and far between in his life since they invariably became demanding of commitment he wasn't willing to make.

"OK. All right. I'll mind my own business," Kay said, laughing good-naturedly. She glanced over at Rusty, now on her knees in the sand and adding the finishing touches to a picturesque sculpture. "I just couldn't pass up this opportunity to point out what a good catch that young woman is. Why, a wife as sensible as she could keep any man—even an overworked business tycoon—grounded."

"And that's what wives are for," Jeffrey said, adding a sly "just ask 'em" that earned him his wife's smart slap on the wrist.

The next instant Kay leaped up from her chair and darted across the sand. Both Reo and Jeffrey stared after her in amazement, trying to find the cause for the sudden move. At once, Reo realized that a brunette holding a baby had joined Rusty and the girls on the beach.

"Why, it's Erin," Jeffrey murmured, standing. He turned to Reo as if on afterthought. "Our neighbor down the beach. She had a baby two weeks ago. Guess she came over to show it, er, *her* to Kay. Can we take five?"

"Uh, sure," Reo answered, motioning his permission for a short break even though he resented the interruption. "Take as long as you like."

Jeffrey joined his wife at once and began to exclaim over the baby held by the woman named Erin. Reo heard such words as *adorable, sweet* and *beautiful*—adjectives he didn't believe could ever honestly be applied to a wrinkled newborn. A few minutes later, to Reo's horror, Rusty took the bundle of joy in her arms and headed his way.

So it was his turn to coo and goo. Damn. Reo barely managed a smile.

"Would you just look at this precious baby?" Rusty said as she sat on the bench beside him.

Grudgingly, Reo did. He saw tiny fingers and toes, ten of each. He saw smooth porcelain skin and a full head of copper-colored hair. He saw perfection. Definitely not as ugly as most babies, this little gal. In fact, she was downright cute—so cute that Reo could easily imagine what a doll she would be at age two or three.

Taking a second to complete the picture that now filled his head, Reo envisioned a sunny day in a park somewhere, a few years in the future. This red-haired baby, now a toddler, played with a frisky puppy in the grass while her parents watched from a bench nearby.

But wait. The mother in this daydream wasn't dark-haired Erin, neighbor of the Moreaus. The mother was Rusty. And the dad—oh, God, the *dad*—was him: Reo Don't-Need-Anyone Sampson.

What a daydream!

No, more like a chilling nightmare. Yet a warm glow spread slowly over his body.

"Her name is Macy." Rusty kissed one of the baby's bare pink toes.

"That's an awfully grown-up name for such a little squirt."

Rusty laughed softly. "She won't always be small."

Reo, who didn't need the reminder, couldn't trust himself to answer.

"Kay says I look more like Macy's mom than Erin does," Rusty continued, looking pleased.

And that, Reo abruptly realized, explained his crazy fantasy. This baby *could* have been Rusty's, so similar was she in coloring. Obviously that, combined with all her talk of children, had kick started his imagination. "You may not have a red-haired baby."

"Well, whatever I have, I'll be crazy about."

"Lucky kid," Reo murmured, experiencing a sharp stab of something very like regret that he wouldn't be around to witness that mother love.

Her gaze met his. For several seconds they just looked at each other, then she got up from the bench and walked over to where the Moreaus still talked with Erin and the girls. A short time later Jeffrey and Kay came back to the table, and work began again.

Focusing on the task at hand, Reo shut his mind to all thoughts of settling down, parenthood and babies. But later, when he lay alone in his bed, everything Kay had said about Rusty that afternoon came back to keep him awake. Reo found himself wondering if there was truth to her comment about wives keeping their husbands "grounded."

His deceased father, who'd lost Reo's mother to cancer early in their marriage, had never walked the aisle again, choosing instead to share the company of secretaries, mistresses and girlfriends. In Reo's opinion, there could never be another man more *disconnected* from the human race.

Was he himself in danger of turning into his dad? he now wondered. And if so, was a woman like Rusty the solution?

Reo wished he knew.

He wished even more that Kay Moreau had never raised the disturbing issue.

Rain threatened all day on Friday. Reo didn't notice, however, since all his attention today was focused on his new business associates, who once again sat with him at the picnic table. This time they brainstormed their idea, as promised.

"I was inspired by the red room upstairs," Kay said with a laugh. "I don't know if you've been in there or not, but the mood is quite—"

"Erotic?" Reo ventured somewhat dryly.

"I was going to say *naughty,* but perhaps *erotic* is more accurate. At any rate, when I couldn't sleep one night, I wandered upstairs and lay on that bed—for a change, you know. I had the strangest dreams, and then Jeff came looking for me, and we—" She broke off, visibly flustered, and glanced at her husband, who looked away and began to whistle softly through his teeth. "Well, it doesn't matter what we did. The bottom line is that we wound up hatching this scheme for a line of lingerie. I have some sketches here. I want you to tell me what you think."

Kay opened the sketch pad she'd been holding and handed it to Reo. With some trepidation—what did he really know about women's lingerie?—he looked at her drawings.

Reo saw panties ranging from thongs to high cut. He saw bras, bustiers and chemises. He saw garter belts, girdles and corsets. And while the garments were familiar enough in design to be recognized for what they were, each piece of clothing bore the unmistakable mark of their talented designer, Kay Moreau.

"I'm thinking franchise," Reo murmured, words that made Kay and Jeffrey exchange a joyful high five. "We'll call our lingerie shop The Red Room."

"Why, that's perfect!" Kay exclaimed. Clearly thrilled, she turned toward the beach. "Rusty! Can you come here for a minute?"

Rusty could and did, joining them at the picnic table.

Quickly Kay explained their idea, including Reo's suggestion of name for their new business venture.

"But aren't there already enough lingerie shops in the malls?" Rusty asked, looking from one to the other of them.

"Show her the drawings," prompted Reo.

Kay handed Rusty the sketch pad. Sitting down next to Reo on the stone bench, Rusty began to peruse the designs.

"These *are* quite unique," she murmured after a minute. Reo noticed that she blushed, a reaction that charmed him. "May I make one suggestion?"

"Fire away," Jeffrey answered, leaning closer so as not to miss a word.

"Don't open a shop at all. Instead, make this a lingerie line that will be offered in existing department stores. You can still call the line The Red Room, but please, please keep everything affordable so middle-class women, like me, can afford to indulge."

"So you'd really wear this stuff?" Reo asked.

"You betcha," she sassily assured him, an answer that hit below the belt.

Reo felt sweat pop out on his forehead and reached for the soft drink given to him earlier.

If Kay and Jeffrey noticed anything amiss, they didn't comment. Rusty wandered back to the sand castles a minute or two later, leaving Reo wishing that the Moreaus had some of Kay's designs already sewn together and that Rusty would volunteer to model them.

Disgusted by the direction his thoughts had taken, Reo then began to wonder if what he felt for Rusty was anything more than physical desire. In truth, the possibility of having sex with her ruled his head—and sometimes his body—whenever she was around. But did that necessarily mean she meant nothing else to him?

Not if yesterday's daydream meant anything.

Up to her knees in sand castles once again, Rusty did a little wondering of her own. She'd seen a decidedly lustful spark in Reo's eye just moments before. She suspected it mirrored a spark in her own, since all she wanted to do today was drag the man upstairs to her marvelous red room and then talk him out of the shockingly casual—for him, anyway—muscle shirt and baggy cotton beach shorts he now wore.

It would be so wonderful, she thought, to be able to forget responsibility and being sensible for just once and indulge in an afternoon of sensual delight. Ah, the memories they'd make—memories that would linger even after they returned to Shreveport, which couldn't be long now.

Rusty's stomach knotted at the thought of going home. Once there, Reo would undoubtedly take cover in his wealthy world, leaving her to cope with her not-so-wealthy one. While she really loved her middle-class life, the realization that she would never see Reo again disturbed her far more than she cared to admit.

During dinner that night, Reo received a phone call from some man named Stiles—a name that Rusty had heard before, but couldn't place. When he returned to the table, he seemed distracted, and she couldn't help but wonder if something bad had happened. It was clear the Moreaus picked up on his mood swing, too. Rusty intercepted more than one curious glance cast Reo's way by adults and children alike.

Minutes later Reo mentioned going home on Saturday. The Moreaus, polite hosts that they were, argued, urging him to stay until Sunday so he could enjoy the beach, something he hadn't really done. Reo hedged his reply, telling them he'd think about it.

After eating, everyone retired to the great room, as usual. Since there was no television, and no other form of entertainment sounded like fun, Rusty suggested a game she made up on the spot and called Twenty-One Questions and a Pop Quiz. Even Reo seemed intrigued when she proposed that they divide into two teams and play.

The rules were simple and silly: each member of the opposing team was allowed to ask seven questions of the person in the spotlight. That person had to answer each as cryptically, but honestly, as possible. Once everyone had answered their twenty-one questions, each team leader got to give the other one a pop quiz based on information shared purposely or inadvertently. Each correct reply earned points. The team with the most correct answers won the game.

Rusty and Reo were named team captains since they were guests. Rusty chose Kayla and Kelsey to be on her side. That left Reo teamed with Kay and Jeffrey. A toss of a coin put Rusty in the spotlight first. Not sure what to expect—she was making this up as they went along—Rusty stood before the fireplace and waited to be questioned.

"When did you get your first kiss?" asked Reo, a question that made the twins giggle.

"When I still lived in Bossier City," replied Rusty with a sweet smile.

Reo winced at that answer, which, while honest enough, told him exactly nothing.

"Obviously we're going to have to be more specific," Jeffrey muttered to his wife.

Kay nodded agreement and asked her first question. "What kind of work do your parents do?"

"My mother is a teacher. My father is a mechanic."

"What's the worst thing you ever did as a child?" asked Jeffrey.

Rusty had to think about that one for a minute. "I cut my sister's hair while she was asleep." Kelsey gasped in horror and glanced over at her rambunctious sibling.

It was Reo's turn again. Grinning, he asked, "Where did you go on your first date?"

"A drive-in movie," Rusty answered.

"What was playing?" Kay asked.

"Um...er...actually, I don't remember." In truth, Rusty hadn't even watched the movie, a fact the other team must have suspected since all three went into fits of laughter. Clearly baffled by the hilarity, Kayla and Kelsey exchanged a wondering look that only made their parents laugh harder.

One by one the questions were asked of Rusty. One by one she answered. Finally they reached number twenty, which felt like one hundred twenty since Rusty had been on the hot seat a full fifteen minutes.

"What kind of wedding do you want?" Kay asked.

"Actually, I've always thought it would be fun to elope to Las Vegas."

"Why, that's what we did!" Kay exclaimed, adding, "And I've never regretted it."

"Neither will I," Rusty said. "And now we're to the last question...thank heaven."

"Make it a good one," Reo advised his team member.

Jeff nodded. "If you had your life to live over, what would you *not* do again?"

Rusty's gaze instantly locked with Reo's. It was evident he thought he knew her answer, but he didn't. Not for anything would Rusty have missed his kiss, his touch. So what if they haunted her forever? At least she knew how it felt to be desired…and by a man who could have anyone he wanted.

Chapter Seven

"Rusty?" prompted Kay, when she didn't answer at once.

"That's a toughie," Rusty admitted, finally naming "Eating that whole box of chocolates last Valentine's," an answer that clearly surprised Reo.

He still looked a bit befuddled when he took the floor to field questions.

Rusty asked the first. "Who was your best friend when you were little?"

"An Irish setter named Finnegan."

No wonder he wanted to meet Bandit.

"What do your parents do?" asked Kayla, probably copying a question her mother had asked earlier.

"Actually, my parents are dead. My mom died when I was seven. My dad died last November." At the stricken look on Kayla's face, he hastened to set her at ease. "It's OK, honey. You didn't know."

Kelsey, no doubt worried about touching on another

sensitive issue, turned to Rusty for guidance. Rusty whispered one of the zillion questions she wanted to ask.

"Do you have a pet now?" asked Kelsey of Reo a moment later.

"Nope."

"Did your dad marry again?" Rusty asked.

"He didn't."

"Then who took care of you?" Kelsey blurted out of turn.

"The housekeeper or, if we didn't have one of those, whoever my dad was dating at the time."

Good grief. Rusty glanced at Kay and Jeffrey, who looked as horrified as she about Reo's unconventional upbringing. No wonder he was such a loner. No wonder he placed business before family. And no wonder he wasn't interested in marrying or having children.

"What do you do for fun?"

Reo grinned, no doubt relieved by Kayla's harmless question. "I play tennis and racquetball, I swim and I jog."

"No golf?" asked Jeffrey, a faux pas that earned him boos from his daughters. "Sorry, sorry. Got caught up. Won't happen again."

"It better not," warned Kayla, shaking her finger at him.

"What's your favorite movie?" asked Rusty, thoughtfully ditching the other personal questions she wanted to ask.

"Swiss Family Robinson."

Now that was an odd choice for a man without relations. Or was he—

Rusty whispered a question to Kayla, who graciously asked it. "Do you have aunts and uncles and cousins?"

"No fair! That's three questions!" Kay said.

"It sure is, but I'm feeling generous," Reo said. "And there's just one answer, anyway. Not that I know of."

What a strange way to phrase that answer. And how on earth did he make it through the day without parents, siblings, aunts, uncles or cousins? Rusty blinked back tears of sympathy that sprang up from nowhere.

"What's your favorite song?" Kelsey asked.

"Who'll Stop the Rain?" he told her, adding, "That's an old song by—"

"Creedence Clearwater Revival," Kayla interjected somewhat scornfully. *"I know."*

"They listen to oldies," Rusty explained.

"Ex-cuse me," Reo murmured, put firmly in his place.

For the next ten minutes, Reo fielded the questions tossed out at him. When he finally sat, Rusty saw the relief on his face and sympathized.

Each of the other team members took their turn in the spotlight, a process that grew shorter as skill was gained. Finally it was time for the seven-question pop quiz. Rusty asked hers first, deliberately choosing the most ordinary, easily-forgotten ones. Then Reo asked his, obviously using the same tactic.

To everyone's surprise, Rusty's team had the most correct answers. After joining in the twins' brief, but noisy, victory celebration, Rusty made her excuses and headed upstairs to shower and go to bed. She fell asleep at once, only to wake a couple of hours later when a gust of wind rattled the panes in her window.

Rusty, who loved storms, got out of bed immediately and ran to look out. Thanks to the intermittent flashes of lightning, she could clearly see the waves that crashed on the shore. A storm approached. No doubt about it.

And Rusty, lover of rain, did not intend to miss a second of the fun.

By now it was after midnight, and the house was silent, sure indication everyone slept. Grabbing her jeans from her suitcase, Rusty slipped into them and then snatched up an afghan off the chair. As soundlessly as is possible in old houses, she crept past Reo's bedroom, down the stairs and out the front door. Her head ducked against the brisk wind, Rusty hurried, barefoot, to the swing, only to stop short when she realized someone occupied it already.

Reo.

At once she turned to go back inside, but he called her name, halting escape, and patted the swing next to him in invitation. Rusty hesitated, not wanting to miss the wild magic of the storm, but not sure she was up to sharing it with a man as potent as Reo.

"Pretend I'm your husband," he coaxed, holding out an arm to her.

She felt his sexy smile to the tips of her bare toes. How much could a poor girl resist? With an answering smile and an I-know-better-but-I'm-doing-this-anyway laugh, Rusty slipped into Reo's warm embrace and spread the afghan over them.

The wind played a crazy, hypnotic tune on the colorful chimes dancing from hooks somewhere behind their heads. Rain pelted the tin roof of the porch—tentative at first, but soon pounding a thunderous rhythm, primitive as any jungle beat. The crash of the waves, the smell of the ocean filled Rusty's head, and, caught up in the sensual fury, she laughed in sheer exhilaration.

Reo laughed, too, and she cuddled closer, glad he was as thrilled as she to be witness to the forceful display. The minutes ticked by. The tempest waned until the moon, just slight of full, could be seen, peeking through the windswept clouds.

Rusty sighed her disappointment that the show was over and tried to slip from Reo's embrace. Instead of letting her go, however, he tightened the hug.

"Got another minute? I-I need to talk."

"I'm here for as long as you need," Rusty told him, an answer straight from the heart.

"I have to make a decision about something," Reo said. "I've got to think out loud."

And he wanted her to be his sounding board? Rusty cherished the honor. "I'm listening."

Reo released her, tossed back the afghan and rose from the swing. He then began to pace the porch. "I got a phone call today from Edward Logan Stiles."

That name again, but Rusty still couldn't place it.

"He's a New Orleans lawyer I hired last week to solve a family mystery. He wants me to stop by his office on our way home tomorrow so he can make his report in person—"

"Then we are leaving tomorrow." Damn.

He nodded. "We'd have plenty of time to see him before the flight."

"If you're asking if I mind a side trip, the answer is no."

"Actually, I'm trying to decide if I should keep the appointment at all. I think I know what he's going to say, and I'm not sure I want to hear it."

Rusty frowned. "Maybe you should start at the beginning. And please sit down, would you? You're making me seasick."

With a sigh Reo plopped back down on the swing. Rusty pushed her rain-damp hair from her eyes and scooted to the opposite end of the bench so she could better focus on her companion. Swinging her feet up, she tucked them under the afghan, then bent her knees so she could hug and rest her chin on them.

"OK…here goes." He hesitated, then plunged ahead. "After my dad died back in November, I decided to put his house up for sale. Naturally I had to go through all his things, and while doing that I came across a contract drawn up just over thirty-five years ago and signed by my grandfather, Randolf Sampson, and some woman named Linette Ashe. According to this contract—which looked legal enough—Linette Ashe agreed to give up all rights to the Sampson fortune in return for a cash payment of ten thousand dollars. Naturally I wondered why this woman, who, it turns out, is a psychic from New Orleans, would have a claim to the Sampson estate in the first place. The only thing I could think of was—"

"—an illicit affair and a pregnancy."

"Exactly," Reo said. "Which means I might have a relative alive and well somewhere."

"Why, Reo, that's wonderful!"

"Yeah…" He frowned.

"You don't seem very pleased."

"Oh, I'm pleased, all right, but I'm more nervous. Damned nervous."

"About what?"

"How this relative is going to feel about me, about this contract. I don't know his or her situation, after all. Illegitimacy is not usually good news."

Rusty winced. "I see your point."

"So do I go see the lawyer, or not?"

"Of course you go see him. And if he doesn't have all the information you need, you hire a private detective, who'll get it for you. Then, if the situation isn't too sticky, you contact this half cousin and tell them the truth.''

''Actually, it's half aunt or uncle.''

Rusty shrugged. ''Whatever. Family is family, and God knows, you could use some.''

''I suppose you're right.''

''Of course I am, and now that we've settled that, *I* need *your* advice.''

''Yeah?'' He arched an eyebrow in surprise. ''About what?''

''The nicknames I'm supposed to give the girls. I've been thinking about them all week, and I'm afraid I've drawn a blank.''

''Let me think for a minute,'' Reo murmured, setting the swing into motion with his foot. For a while Rusty heard nothing but the steady creak of the chain, the drip drip of the rain, and the crash of the waves. Hypnotizing sounds, those, and they almost put her to sleep before Reo's sudden ''I've got it!''

Rusty nearly fell off the swing. ''Names?''

''One, anyway. Kayla's the leader of the two, don't you think?''

''Mmm-hmm.''

''Then why don't you call her Scout?''

Scout...Scout. Rusty mulled over the name for several seconds. ''I like it. Now what about Kelsey?''

''Kelsey isn't so easy.'' He sat in silence for several more moments. ''I see her as steady, thorough and careful.''

''Very good,'' Rusty murmured, amazed at his perception until she remembered he was an astute businessman, after all, and probably skilled at sizing people up. ''But do we want to focus on those qualities? I mean, they sound sort of dull.''

"Too dull for a sprite like Kelsey," Reo agreed.

"Sprite! That's it." Rusty lowered her feet to the floor and slipped off the swing. "Thanks, Reo. You've saved me. Now I'm going to bed before I fall asleep, fall off this swing and break a bone. Unless you have another problem you'd like me to solve...."

"None I'm willing to talk about," he replied, standing again. "Good night, Rusty." He kissed the top of her head.

"'Night, Reo," she responded, lightly tracing the Sampson Enterprises logo on his T-shirt with her finger. Moments later they parted in the upstairs hall and went to their separate bedrooms.

Saturday dawned so brightly that the storm seemed like a dream. Rusty rose a bit earlier than usual, and, enlisting artist Kay's aid, created a surprise for the girls.

When everyone gathered for breakfast, Rusty ushered them out on the patio instead, for the christening ceremony she'd promised the twins. After instructing Reo, Jeffrey and Kay to sit on the bench that belonged to the picnic table, Rusty motioned for Kayla and Kelsey to join her by a potted palm. She then slipped inside the house to get the surprises Kay had created for her daughters.

"Who's the oldest?" Rusty asked the girls when she walked back outside moments later. She kept the hand holding the surprises tucked behind her back.

"Me," answered Kayla.

"Then I'll rename you first." With her free hand, Rusty motioned for Kayla to join her near the plant. "Reo helped me with your nicknames. The one we picked for you is Scout. We're naming you that because you like to lead the way."

Clearly pleased, Kayla grinned at her mother and daddy.

"In honor of your new name, your mother painted this for you," Rusty then said, handing Kayla a piece of poster board with her new nickname spelled out on it in fancy green lettering surrounded by flowers, seashells and butterflies—all the things she loved. No one could doubt Kayla's delight. "And now it's your turn, Kelsey."

Kelsey hopped into place.

"Reo and I are calling you Sprite. Do you know what a sprite is?"

Kelsey shook her head.

"A sprite is sort of like a fairy. You're every bit as special as that and even more."

"Thank you," said Kelsey, smiling shyly.

"Here's your painting," Rusty said, handing the girl her poster. Sprite was written on it in purple, and the background featured fairies of all shapes and sizes.

A noisy breakfast followed, during which the girls tried out their nicknames. Shortly after, Reo loaded up the car. Many hugs and goodbyes later, he and Rusty left their friends at Driftwood Bay.

The two of them said little on the drive to New Orleans. Rusty, somewhat depressed after the emotional parting with the Moreau twins, stared out the window. Reo concentrated on the road.

The clock on the dash said 10:30 when he drove their rented car into a parking lot beside an old, but well-maintained, red brick building. Reo killed the engine yet made no move to get out of the vehicle until Rusty nudged him on the shoulder with her hand. Then he gave her a half smile and climbed out.

Only when he walked around the car and opened her

door, did Rusty realize Reo intended that she accompany him inside. Surprised, she nonetheless acquiesced. If the man needed moral support, then she would definitely give it.

The office of Edward Logan Stiles proved to be plush and beautifully decorated. Reo and Rusty sat in the waiting room barely five minutes before the receptionist came out and escorted them down a hall to an office. A portly gray-haired man greeted them cordially, introduced himself as Edward Stiles, then showed them to overstuffed tweed chairs. Stepping behind a massive mahogany desk, he sat facing them.

"As I said on the phone, I've unraveled some of the mystery surrounding this contract. It wasn't hard to do…in fact, a trip to the courthouse and a couple of phone calls solved the whole thing. There are still some unanswered questions, but I must say, most of your theories have proved to be correct."

"Then my grandfather did have an affair with this Ashe woman?"

"Actually, it was your father, Jon Sampson, who was involved with Linette Ashe, which makes her children your half siblings."

The color drained from Reo's face. "*Children*…as in more than one?"

"Linette Ashe gave birth to twins—a boy and a girl—March eleventh, thirty-five years ago. I feel certain I can locate them, Mr. Sampson, if they're still living, of course, and if you want me to."

Rusty, unable to contain her excitement at the good news, reached out and clutched Reo's arm. "Of course he wants you to," she told Stiles. "Don't you, Reo?"

"Actually, I need to think about it."

"*Think about it?*" Only when Reo glared at Rusty

did she remember this wasn't really her business. At once she released him and sat back in the chair, hands folded demurely in her lap.

"I understand," Edward Stiles said, as though people denied the existence of kin every day. Rusty couldn't believe her ears.

"I'll call you in a couple of days," Reo said, standing.

Feeling somewhat dazed by what she'd heard, Rusty rose from her chair and followed Reo out the door. Once in the car again, she could only stare at him, dumbfounded.

He ignored her, and not a word was spoken until they settled themselves into their seats on the plane. Then Rusty could hold her peace no longer.

"Is money the issue?" she blurted. "Are you afraid that your brother and sister might want a share of your father's estate?"

"Damn, Rusty," he retorted, clearly angry. "Will you give me a break here? I just learned that some woman somewhere gave birth to twins barely *three months* before my mother gave birth to me. That makes my dad a bigger bastard than I ever dreamed, and I'm having a little trouble dealing with it, OK?"

"Oh, God, Reo. I didn't realize—"

"Yeah, well, I can tell you this—if my old man were alive today, I'd...I'd..." Abruptly he broke off and stared out the window, fists clenched, face flushed.

Rusty, wishing she'd kept her big mouth shut, simply didn't know what to say, so said nothing.

"It's not the money," he said after a few moment's silence.

"Of course not," she quickly agreed, embarrassed to have ever thought that.

"I haven't taken a penny from Jon Sampson since I

turned twenty-one and came into the trust established for me by my mother, who had her own money. I bought Sampson Enterprises from him then, and he moved on to bigger and better things.''

"You don't have to tell me this.''

"I want you to understand it isn't greed that's keeping me from calling up those people. They can have everything that old man had. Everything.''

"'Those people' are your family, Reo,'' Rusty said.

"Maybe I don't want a family,'' he answered, words that shocked her. "Maybe I've been alone so long that I like it.''

"You can't be serious.''

"I am, and if you have trouble believing it, well, maybe you don't know me at all.''

"Apparently I don't.''

As irritated as she was disconcerted, Rusty snatched a magazine from the holder on the back of the seat in front of her and pretended to read. Reo looked out the window, even though there was nothing to see but clouds.

Once they landed, Reo wasted no time in deboarding, politely letting Rusty lead the way.

"You did a good job for me,'' he said, offering his right hand as any short-term boss might do. Rusty felt awkward when she took and shook it, more like some stranger instead of a foolish woman whose bare breasts he'd tasted. "Payroll will be sending you a check in a couple of days.''

"Thanks,'' she somehow replied. "May I, um, use you for a reference if I need to?''

"Anytime.''

An awkward silence followed those niceties, then Rusty turned and walked away. "See ya,'' she called over her shoulder as she moved on, gaining speed with every step. By the time Rusty reached the door, she as good as ran, but she didn't care. The sooner she put distance between herself and Reo, the happier she'd be.

In fact, if she never saw him again it would be OK. No, even better than OK. It would be wonderful.

"Hey, girl," Jade greeted Rusty when she walked in her front door a quarter hour later.

Rusty could barely hear her housemate, thanks to the blaring stereo and the chatter of what looked to be at least twenty or more guests in the middle of a swinging party. Outside, Bandit barked to be let back in.

"Come join the fun. Casey's here, and Mark, too." Jade winked slyly at Rusty and beckoned for her to come along to the den.

"I think I'll pass," Rusty answered. "I'm really tired." Not to mention a little irritated about having to park down the street. Sometimes Jade was a tad inconsiderate.

"Sure?" The brunette had begun to move to the music, dancing with an invisible partner.

"Positive," answered Rusty, heading down the hall to her bedroom. Once there, she made short work of unpacking and slipping into a sweatshirt handed down from one of her brothers and a pair of faded jeans.

Rusty stretched out on the bed for a while and tried to read a book. Concentration proved impossible. All she could think about was never seeing Reo again, and her spirits sank lower and lower with every passing minute.

He needed her. True, he didn't know it, but he needed her, he really did. To teach him about giving. To teach him about love. To teach him about wives, children, families—the things that counted most in this world.

Life lessons such as those would take time. While she felt sure she could talk Reo out of his time, she felt equally sure he would use it to attempt a little teaching of his own. Could she hold firm to her ideals, to her dreams? Or, blinded by his charm, would she lose sight of her goals?

Clearly there were risks involved. Clearly she'd be wise to do as she'd always done: wait for a man who *already* valued what she valued. But what if he didn't come? What if she waited and waited—something few women did these days—and he never showed up. Wasn't that a risk, too? Suddenly lonesome, Rusty honestly believed this second risk to be even greater than the first.

Shaking off her doldrums, she rolled off the bed and walked back up the hall to the kitchen to retrieve a piece of the chocolate cake she hoped was still in the refrigerator. Nothing could cheer up this gloomy girl better, in her opinion, nothing except a flesh-and-blood man named Reo, that is.

More than one guest called out a greeting, and Rusty waved to acknowledge all. Just as she opened the refrigerator door, the phone rang. Rusty answered the one on the kitchen wall, covering her free ear with her hand to block the party commotion. "Hello."

"Is Rusty there?" It was Reo, and her heart jumped for joy.

"This is Rusty."

"Reo, here. Sounds like I called at a bad time."

"Jade's having a party."

"Ah, well, I just wanted to thank you again. You were fantastic this week. The Moreaus commented on it more than once."

"I had a great time."

"Good…good." He sounded uncomfortable, almost

as if he'd actually wanted to say something else altogether.

"Is that why you really called? To thank me again?"

"Yes, er, actually no, not really. I called because I miss you—"

Yeeesss!

"—and I was thinking I'd like to get to know you on a more personal level."

More personal than they'd already been? Criminy! "I'm free now."

"You weren't invited to Jade's party?"

"I was, but I declined."

"Can you be ready in thirty minutes?"

"I can be ready in ten."

"Good. Dress casual."

"In that case," she said, "I'm ready now."

Exactly nineteen minutes later, Rusty waved at Reo to keep him from walking up to the porch, and ran down her sidewalk to get into his sleek blue Jaguar.

"I was coming to the door," Reo told her, slipping back behind the steering wheel.

"You can do it twice next time," Rusty answered, foolishness that made him chuckle.

She tried not to stare at him, but couldn't help it. Dressed in tattered jeans and a plain white T-shirt— something she'd never dreamed he'd wear out—he looked good enough to kidnap.

"OK if we go to the park?"

"Parking is fine with me," Rusty told him.

Reo chortled this time, a full-bodied sound that made her smile. "God, I'm glad I called you. You wouldn't believe how down I was when I got home."

"Hey, I'm always good for a laugh."

"My personal joker?" He gave her a wry smile.

"Tonight, anyway," she said.

"What if it's not a joker I need, but a friend?"

"I can be a friend, too, Reo."

"And what if it's not a friend I need, but a lover?" he asked even as he turned the car into a small parking lot next to a public jogging trail. The minute he killed the motor, he turned in the seat. "Forget I said that, will ya? I know you want more than sex on a regular basis."

"Actually, sex on a regular basis sounds heavenly right now," Rusty admitted. Being good was seldom easy. With this man in this car, it was impossible.

"It does?" He frowned his disbelief.

"It does," Rusty answered, shutting her mind to reason and closing the distance between them.

Chapter Eight

Reo met Rusty halfway, hugging her hard and then kissing her with a hunger that only served to whet her own appetite. Once, twice, three times they kissed—each deeper, wetter, longer than the last. Rusty skimmed her fingernails over his back, producing a shiver so violent he caught his breath. In response, he began a sensual onslaught that began with his suckling her earlobe and ended with his suckling her breast.

Luckily there was only one other car in the lot, and it, empty. Rusty didn't have the strength to resist him and wouldn't have, even if there had been witnesses to their passion. She flicked her tongue over his chin, touched it to the pulse pounding in his neck, then dipped lower to tease his nipples taut.

"Ah, Rusty," he murmured with a groan, a second before he tensed and caught her head in his hands. "Someone's coming."

Well, darn. Rusty raised her mouth from his bare chest and twisted around to see. Sure enough, another car had turned into the lot. Hastily she straightened her clothing. Reo did the same, then started the powerful motor, backed the car and peeled out of the lot. Only when they reached the stop sign at the end of the block did he speak.

"Your place or mine?"

"There's a party at my house, remember?"

"Then it's mine."

Rusty laid her head back on the seat and closed her eyes during the trip, highly aware of the fact that her bra was still unfastened under her sweatshirt, and her jeans were half-unzipped. Still a bit dazed from Reo's skilled lovemaking, she refused to think about what she was doing now and didn't even notice her surroundings until he pulled up to an enormous iron gate and spoke into an intercom. Slowly the gates opened. Reo put the car in motion again, not stopping until they reached the four-car garage of the biggest estate Rusty had ever seen in her life.

"What's this?" she blurted out, for a second actually wondering if he'd decided to take her to some posh hotel instead of his house.

"My place."

"Damn, Reo." The words were spoken in respect— utter awe, really. Never, ever had she imagined he lived in a house like this...not even in her worst nightmares. Reality was like a much-needed splash of cold water right in her flushed face. "I-I can't go in there."

"Why in the devil not?"

"It's too big."

"Don't be ridiculous," he retorted, getting out of the car, walking around it to open Rusty's door.

But instead of climbing out, she just shook her head

and fought for composure. "I think I've made a mistake. I think I'd better just go home."

"You're kidding, right?"

"Wrong. I want to go home...please take me now."

"But—"

"Please, Reo." Rusty bit her quivering lip to keep from bursting into tears.

Reo, who obviously saw her distress, hesitated for barely a heartbeat before he got back into the car and started the engine. He drove her home quickly and in silence, parking in the only spot he could—several houses down from Rusty's place, where Jade's party still thrived.

Rusty reached to open the door, a move Reo halted by catching her hand in his. "Talk to me, Rusty."

"I don't know what to say," she answered, looking at the radio, the floor mat, the ceiling—everything but her companion.

"Start by telling me what's wrong with my house."

"It's not a house, it's a mansion, which is exactly what's wrong with it."

"So before you knew where I lived, I was acceptable as a lover?"

Rusty sighed and shook her head. "I'm not sure I would've gone through with this. I mean, something else would probably have brought me to my senses before I...before we..." She stammered to a halt. "You think I'm a tease, and I deserve it. This isn't the first time I've backed out, after all."

"I don't think you're a tease," Reo answered with a heavy sigh. "I think you're a woman who doesn't know what she wants."

"But I do know what I want," Rusty argued. "I simply forget when I'm with you because…because…oh, I don't know why. I just do."

"I can tell you why." His voice, silky soft in the dark, shimmied down her spine. "You forget because I make you *feel*, which has nothing to do with common sense or logic or stupid dreams. Well, I want you to know that you make me feel, too, Rusty. And that feeling is something I don't want to give up."

"Well, you're going to have to. We come from two different worlds. And, as the saying goes, 'East is east, and west is w—'"

Reo's kiss smothered the rest of the quote, reminding her that east and west melded with a blinding flash every time their lips touched. Reo's words brought the reminder home. "The 'twain' just met, darlin', and I dare you to tell me you didn't like it."

Rusty didn't take him up on the dare, instead shrugging and looking away.

"I'm a successful businessman with good prospects and a hell of a lot of money—an 'A-prime bachelor,' I believe Kay Moreau said. Most women would jump at the chance to be with a guy like me. Why do you resist?"

"I'm resisting because the very assets most women admire are the ones that scare me away," Rusty answered. "I want to be everything to the man in my life, Reo, just as my mother has always been to my dad, and just as my sister never was to her rich husband. You're just like my brother-in-law…just like him. You need no special person in your life, no family. Why, you can't even decide if you want to get to know your own brother and sister."

Reo winced.

"And why is that?" Rusty continued. "I'll tell you

why… Because you have too many other *things* to keep you happy. You don't need your family. You don't need me.''

Reo sighed and dropped his head back on the neck rest. ''I admit I get carried away with work sometimes, but the rewards are wealth and position, something you could benefit from if you play your cards right.''

''Wealth and position are hindrances in my eyes…detractors from what matters most—marriage and children.''

''Look, Rusty. All I want is a sexual relationship with a woman I greatly admire. I'm not cut out for 'I do,' so can you please forget the marriage stuff for a minute and give my proposal some honest consideration?''

''Proposal, my foot. That was a proposition, and my answer to it is no. You're incapable of putting me or any woman first in your life. You'd rather relegate them to a neat little folder labeled 'Pleasure,' located after 'Business,' but before 'Sleep' in the file box of your life.''

''Clever. Real clever.''

''And the last thing I'm saying to you tonight or ever,'' Rusty as good as shouted, scrambling out of the car, slamming the door.

Teeth clenched, Reo watched her run down the street and then up her sidewalk to her, thankfully, lit porch. She had to pound on the front door for several seconds with her fists before it was opened, which irritated the heck out of him.

Only when she disappeared into the house did Reo start up the car and drive away. It was cold shower time again, it seemed, but he didn't fault Rusty for the fact.

How could he when he was just as confused as she?

Instead of heading straight home, Reo stopped at the

health club he preferred and submitted his body to a punishing workout on the Universal machines. Over an hour passed before he got back into his car and drove to his house, physically improved, but still an emotional wreck.

A man used to dealing quickly with problems when they arose, Reo didn't know where to begin solving the ones looming largest in his life right now. Should he tell Stiles to go ahead and locate his brother and sister? Most people would, but then most people weren't Reo Sampson—son of a heartless business magnate who disdained familial ties.

Had the ol' man always been so cruel, so cold? Reo wondered as he tossed down his car keys and stared at an old photo of his mother, framed and hanging on the wall in a place of honor. Sarah had doted on his dad. Other old photos and his own sharp memories proved that.

Surely if a woman sweet as Sarah could love Jon Sampson, he couldn't have been all bad. They'd been high school sweethearts, for Pete's sake. She probably knew him better than anyone else, and he, her. Yet he'd slept with another woman mere months before his wedding, damn him. Slept with her and fathered twins, then taken the coward's way out.

The coward's way out? And wasn't that exactly what Reo Sampson now considered a viable option…the coward's way out? Like father, like son, it seemed.

Or maybe not.

Reo strode to his grandfather's massive desk and sat down. As he'd done not so many days ago, he picked up a piece of paper and, with a pen, drew a bold black line down the center of it.

He labeled one column "Pros" and the other "Cons"

and then, under each, began to list reasons—excuses, really—for not trying to find his long-lost relatives. There were several under "Cons": shame—both his and theirs—embarrassment, inconvenience, uncertainty. There was only one under "Pros": blood kin.

What, exactly, did blood kin mean? Not much to him, he admitted, though it obviously meant plenty to Rusty, to the Moreaus and to a lot of other people he knew— good people with their heads on straight and their hearts in the right places.

His heart was in the right place, or so he'd always thought. A big donor to a lot of worthy causes, Reo considered himself a generous man. So why did his heart now feel so cold? Could it be he was turning into his dad?

God help him.

Coming to an abrupt decision, Reo reached for the phone, only to discover it wasn't where it was supposed to be. He looked around for several minutes, thoroughly baffled, before he remembered stashing it in the drawer to keep from calling Rusty. Retrieving the desk key from the vase where he'd hidden it, Reo had to laugh.

A lot of good his hiding the phone had done him.

Edward Stiles answered on the second ring and didn't seem a bit irritated that Reo had utilized his business card and called the emergency number. He also didn't seem a bit surprised when Reo gave him the go-ahead to find his half siblings. They talked for several minutes, Stiles sharing his plans to hire a private detective to do the actual work of locating the twins. Before the conversation was terminated, the lawyer promised to call Reo as soon as he received any information, hopefully a matter of days.

Reo felt as if the weight of the world had been lifted

from his shoulders when he hung up the phone. Exhilarated, he glanced at the clock, noting that it was just after eleven, then passed several moments wondering if it was too late to call Rusty and tell her what he'd done.

In the end, he decided it wasn't, but a machine answered the call. Though Reo suspected Rusty might be screening her calls, he left a request for her to get back to him as soon as possible, something he could only pray she would actually do.

"So how was your day?" Jade asked when Rusty got home on Friday of the following week. The brunette sat at the table, clipping grocery coupons from the past Sunday's newspaper—her one and only domestic skill.

"A killer," Rusty answered, setting a box of birthday party gear on the table and slipping her overloaded purse off her shoulder. "My feet will never be the same."

"Today must have been zoo day."

"Yeah." She glanced toward the answering machine. "Any calls?"

"Just the usual six from *Re-o*." Jade sort of sang the last word, rolling her eyes in disgust. "Are you ever going to call that man back?"

"Nope."

"And just why not?"

"We don't have anything in common."

"Oh, but you do, girl—money. His overabundance and your lack of."

"Very funny." Rusty grabbed a diet drink from the refrigerator and headed down the hall to the bathroom, where she quickly stepped out of her clothes and into a hot shower. After that, hair wrapped in a towel, she went to her bedroom and began the tedious process of detangling her natural curls while she watched—or, rather, listened to—the evening news. Bent over so that her hair almost touched the floor, Rusty couldn't really see the television.

Just as the weather report started, Jade knocked on the doorjamb. "You had a call while you were showering."

"I didn't hear the phone ring," Rusty said, straightening up and tossing her hair back so she could see Jade, standing in the doorway. Rusty got her diet soda from the dresser and took a swallow.

"Well, it did, and I answered." Jade raised a hand to ward off her friend's disapproval. "*After* I screened the call, of course." She handed Rusty a phone number. "A prospective customer."

"Oh, good," Rusty murmured, laying the card on the bed.

"Aren't you going to call him back?"

"It's a him?"

"Yes," Jade said. "A frantic father. I told him you wouldn't be but a minute."

"Then I guess I won't be," Rusty grumbled, picking up the card and her telephone. She punched out the number with exaggerated speed, before sticking out her tongue at Jade, who could be so irritating....

Her housemate just laughed and left.

The phone rang on the other end. Reo Sampson answered.

"Well, hell!" Rusty exclaimed and hung up the phone—or almost did. His cry stopped her right before she dropped the receiver in the cradle.

"Don't hang up!"

Slowly Rusty raised the receiver to her ear. She'd known she wouldn't be able to resist him, the reason she'd been screening all calls the past week.

"Rusty? Are you there?"

"I'm here," she murmured, sinking down to perch on the edge of the bed.

"Thank God." She heard him take a deep breath. "I didn't know what I was going to do if you hung up on me."

"Get on with your life, maybe?"

"Life isn't worth living without you."

"What?"

"You heard me. Look, Rusty, I'm sorry I hurt you. I swear I won't do it again."

"No, you won't, because we're not going to see each other anymore."

"But I miss you."

Rusty fell back on the bed. "You do?"

"I swear I do, and I want you in my life."

Oh, Lord. "I really have to go now, Reo." She barely managed the words.

"You can't go. I haven't said everything I need to say."

There was more? "I-I don't have time to talk to you. I have to go buy a birthday present for my brothers."

"Great. I'll meet you there."

"You don't even know where I'm going."

"I will when you tell me, babe."

Babe? Darn, but the man knew just what to say to turn her brain to mush. "Super Sales. I'm going to Super Sales."

"Where's that?" he asked, not surprising since he'd probably never shopped at a discount store.

"Across from South Park Mall."

"I'll find it. Where will you be?"

"In sporting goods. The woman with the freckles and stringy red hair."

"I think your hair is beautiful, Rusty. As for those freckles…I'd love to kiss each one."

Holy!— Muttering a hasty "Later," Rusty dropped the receiver into the cradle and snatched up a pillow to hide her flaming face.

"Are you going to meet him?" Jade had materialized from nowhere and now snatched the covering from her head.

"Of course," Rusty answered. "Heaven help me."

"Well, hot dam-a-lam!" her housemate said, dancing a little jig out the door.

Reo spotted Rusty at once, standing by some camouflage-colored life vests, her back to him. Dressed in boots, leggings and an oversize cotton sweater, she was every man's dream—his most of all. He eased up behind her, quickly and quietly as possible, slipping his arms around her waist when he reached her.

"Boo!" he said softly, right in her ear.

She never jumped, but just leaned against him for half a second before prying his hug loose. "None of that. All we're going to do is talk."

"Yes, ma'am," he murmured, stepping obediently back, hands in the air stick-'em-up style. He looked at the life vests hanging on a rack in front of them. "Why would anyone need one of these in this color?" he asked, since in his experience life jackets were only worn while waterskiing or maybe fishing.

"So the ducks won't see the hunter, silly," Rusty replied, reaching up and selecting two, sized XXL.

Of course. "So your brothers are duck hunters."

She began to move toward the checkout counter. "Uh-huh, and I take it you aren't."

"No, but I wouldn't mind trying that particular sport," he answered, tagging along.

"Maybe Bit or Spin will teach you."

Reo liked the sound of that. It indicated a future of some kind—his goal tonight. Patiently he stood by Rusty while she paid the salesclerk, got her merchandise and then turned to him.

"So where do you want to go to talk? And it better be public...."

"You pick."

"The Yogurt Shoppe." She tilted her head to one side and waited for his answer.

"Well, I'm not wild about yogurt—" actually he hated it "—but if you want some, I'm game."

"This is frozen yogurt," Rusty told him. "If you like ice cream, then you'll love this and save tons of calories."

"Then the Yogurt Shoppe it is."

Minutes later found them seated at a table for two at the nearby confectionery, sharing the biggest, best banana split Reo had ever tasted. "You're sure this is low calorie?" he asked around a chilly bite. His teeth ached from the cold.

"It was until we added the chocolate sauce, whipped cream and nuts," Rusty answered with a laugh.

"You know I wasn't lying when I said life wasn't worth living without you."

Rusty nearly choked, probably due to the sudden switch in topics.

"I want you to move in with me," Reo continued, leaning closer, capturing her wrists in his hands. The spoon she still held dripped yogurt onto the back of her other hand. In one quick move that couldn't have been noticed by anyone, Reo licked it off. Rusty nearly fell off her chair.

"S-so I should just pack up my current life, haul it over to your place and store it in your attic?" Clearly he'd disconcerted her.

"I'm not asking you to 'store' your current life. I just thought it would be easier if you came to live with me since I'm not that fond of Jade."

"You mean *you'd* move in with *me* if I didn't have a housemate?"

"Absolutely."

"That's crazy."

Reo tightened his grip on her wrists. "I'll do anything to have you and to keep you. I'm a desperate man."

Rusty calmly twisted free of his hold and laid down her plastic spoon. "Define *desperate*."

"I can't concentrate on my work, and I'm so grouchy that Angie actually threatened to quit today."

Her frown said she doubted his sincerity.

"I can't sleep, either," he continued earnestly. "I have no energy. I'm—"

"Lying?"

Damn. "No. I'm trying to make you understand that if you'll let me into your life, I'll do my level best to be everything you want in a man."

Rusty sighed. "If you have to change to be what I want, then you aren't the man for me, Reo. Can't you see that? Neither of us should have to change for the other. We should be suited from the start. I want to get married and have children. You don't. We...are... not...a...match."

"Sometimes affairs result in weddings." There, he'd done it—admitted that a walk down the aisle was no longer on his list of fates worse than death. Did Rusty understand the magnitude of the admission?

Her wide eyes said she did.

"So what do you say?" he softly prompted.

"I say...I say *our* affair probably wouldn't. You aren't even interested in getting to know your half brother and sister, all the family you have. How can I possibly hope you'll ever be interested in tying the knot with me and starting a family of your own?"

So that was it. Reo leaned back in his chair and grinned. "I forgot to tell you that I called Stiles last Saturday night and told him to proceed with the search for my family."

Rusty pressed a hand to her heart as if it were about to jump out of her chest. "You swear?"

"I swear."

"Oh, Reo, I'm so proud of you." She grabbed both his hands and squeezed them in hers.

"So you see you may not know me as well as you think you do."

"Maybe I don't," she admitted. "And maybe you don't know me as well as you think, either."

"Probably not. What say we spend some time together, get to know each other better?"

"You mean date for a while instead of sharing a roof right away?"

She sounded so thoughtful, he leaped on the compromise. "Yeah. That's exactly what I mean." He raised her hands to his mouth and kissed the back of each. "You and I could have something special. We owe it to ourselves to work this thing out."

"To teach each other...."

"Then you'll go out with me?"

"On one condition. No sex. I want to see if we can be friends."

Reo swallowed his disappointment in a noisy gulp. "Agreed. Now, I'm having a dinner party tomorrow night—six people, not counting you and me, most of them business acquaintances. Will you come?"

"If you'll come to my brothers' birthday party on Sunday at my parents' house. There'll be—" she counted quickly on her fingers "—twenty there, and I am counting you."

"I'll come. So it's settled?"

"Not until you tell me what to wear to this dinner party."

"Wear anything, wear nothing."

"Reo..." Her tone warned, but her eyes twinkled.

"A dress. That green one you wore to Sartoni's will be perfect."

"Hmm. Well, you should come casual on Sunday. In fact, those jeans you had on last Saturday night would probably be best. I'm sure my brothers will challenge you to a game of cutthroat volleyball—to measure your suitability as a boyfriend, you know."

Reo gave her a wry grin. "Thanks for the warning."

"It's the least I could do," Rusty told him with a smile that probably wasn't as innocent as it looked.

Rusty actually wore something different to Reo's the next night, choosing, instead, a soft peach sweater and a flippy skirt hemmed several inches above the knee. Square-toed pumps completed the outfit, which Jade pronounced "Perfect!" to set Rusty's insecurities to rest.

Her hand shook when she raised it to ring Reo's doorbell that night. He answered the door himself, successfully shattering the first of her preconceived notions of

how the rich and famous entertained—she'd expected a
maid or butler in uniform to do the honors.

Reo ushered her into a beautifully decorated den and
then left her there alone—she'd come a little early at his
request—for so long that she finally trailed him to the
kitchen. To her surprise, he was actually cooking the
meal, thereby shattering expectation number two—a
gourmet chef, complete with ridiculous white hat and
starched jacket.

"Do you cook often?" she had to ask, sniffing the
savory air. Reo had relegated her to a bar stool to watch,
even though she'd offered to help.

"Only if there's someone besides me here. Cooking
for one is a drag."

"So if we cohabited, you'd pull KP?"

"You betcha, schweethardt," he answered, waltzing
by—tomato in one hand, knife in the other—to plant a
hot kiss right on her mouth.

Chapter Nine

Rusty nearly fainted. At that moment the doorbell rang.

"Why don't I get it," she offered, slipping off the stool and right out of the kitchen in her eagerness for a little fresh air. She caught her breath at the door, counted to five, and then opened it, a welcoming smile pasted on her face. "Hello. Come in. I'm Rusty Hanson, a friend of Reo's."

"So you're Rusty," answered the gray-haired woman who stepped into the foyer, followed by a white-haired man. Her gaze swept Rusty from head to toe. "I've heard so much about you."

"You have?"

"Yes, indeed." The woman smiled and offered her hand. "I'm Martha Crain. This is my husband, Leo. We've known Reo since he was a baby. His mother, Sarah, and I were very close."

"Oh. Well, it's great to meet you both. Please come on in. Reo's in the kitchen." She walked them to the den, where she expected them to sit and make small talk.

Instead they headed right into the kitchen as if they'd been there many times before. Rusty could only sigh and follow, tossing out the rest of her preformed ideas about habits of the wealthy. Obviously she didn't know as much as she thought.

The guests continued to arrive in twos, until all six found their way to the kitchen, fortunately a spacious room. Several volunteered to assist, and Reo let them, a fact that rankled.

"You turned down my offer of help," she said.

"That's because you're special," Reo answered, looking for all the world like he might kiss her again, interested witnesses or no.

Rusty took a quick step back, an action that earned her several raised eyebrows and knowing smiles. Clearly these people thought she and Reo were having an affair, an arrangement they probably found acceptable, maybe even fashionable. Well, Rusty believed a more permanent association was most popular with the middle class. And she only hoped she could win Reo over to her way of thinking.

During the next hour Rusty relaxed in spite of herself and began to lose the feelings of inadequacy and inferiority that had originally threatened her good time. She met Ann Bradley, a mother of two who, though married to a prominent physician named Joe, continued to teach school because she loved it. That was an eye-opener to Rusty, who'd assumed these women spent their days planting irises or playing tennis at a country club somewhere.

Rusty also met Phyllis Morrison, a secretary and the fiancée of Sampson Enterprises' corporate attorney, Les Carson. It took one carefully worded question to find out that Phyllis and Les were *not* already living together, and just one more to find out their wedding was going to be as "small" as was possible when a bride had six siblings.

Rusty learned other things: Leo struggled with arthritis; Joe currently sought a partner so he could spend more time with his kids; Les drove to Texarkana, Arkansas, every Sunday to visit his mother in a nursing home.

So these people had jobs and problems, good times and bad, just like the so-called normal people with whom Rusty usually associated. What a concept! And before the party ended, she felt a total fool for having so many ridiculous prejudices.

Finally the last guest left. Reo shut the door and turned to her, clearly anxious. "Did you have a good time?"

"I had a great time, actually," she assured him, taking his hand and leading him to the den. She sat on the love seat and motioned for him to join her. "And that means I'd better apologize."

"Yeah? For what?" he asked as he sat.

"For being such a snob. You were right. I was wrong. All people really are the same deep down inside."

He smiled, obviously pleased, but said nothing.

"Now it's very late, so I think we'd better get started on those dishes."

"Leave 'em, leave 'em. The maid will clean up the kitchen tomorrow."

"You have a maid?" Rusty questioned, ready to eat every word she'd just uttered.

Reo threw his head back and laughed at her outrage. "Nah. But I do have a lady who comes in and cleans for me every two weeks. Tomorrow is her day, lucky woman."

"That's mean."

"I'll pay her double." He got up and walked over to the CD player and punched a button. Immediately the sexy wail of a saxophone filled the air. "Want to dance?"

"I don't think so," Rusty answered, knowing full well where that might lead.

"Aw, come on," he coaxed, taking her hand, pulling her to her feet. A heartbeat later found her held tightly in his arms, her cheek pressed to his, swaying to the music. He brushed his lips over her face, his hands over her back and hips. Rusty felt her resolve melting…melting…and couldn't resist molding her body to his. "I have some etchings in my bedroom upstairs that I'd love to show you."

"I'm not into etchings," she answered, closing her eyes, cherishing the smell and feel of him. Lordy, but the man could move.

"Well, then, how about we take a midnight swim in my pool. It's heated."

"I'm too warm already."

A long silence followed that reply. Then he tried again. "Want to drive to Cross Lake and count submarines?"

"If I drive anywhere, it's going to be home. Give it up, Reo. I'm not going to get physical with you tonight."

He sighed. "Can't blame a guy for trying."

"And you can't blame a gal for wanting something that will last a little longer."

Reo stopped their dance and released Rusty, then framed her face in his hands. "This seems like the perfect time to tell you that what I have in mind for us will last years and years. I'm half in love with you, Rusty, maybe even three-fourths, and that's a first for me."

"I care about you, too, Reo, which is why I'm so scared. I don't want to be hurt."

"I'd never hurt you."

"Not on purpose, no." Taking his hands from her face, Rusty retrieved her purse and headed for the front door.

"You're leaving?" Reo demanded, hurrying after her.

"I am." Noting the disappointment on his face, she leaned close, brushed her lips over his and smiled. "I'll pick you up at one o'clock tomorrow, OK?"

"OK," he answered, giving her a smile that didn't reach his eyes. It was all Rusty could do to leave him, but somehow she did—running to her car, backing down the drive before she gave in to her raging hormones and his.

Reo took one look at the people milling around Mr. and Mrs. Hanson's backyard the next day and wanted to crawl under a rock somewhere. As if sensing his disquiet, Rusty squeezed the hand she held and led him right into the fray.

"Mom, Dad, this is Reo Sampson," she said, releasing his hand so she could give him a little push forward. "Reo, this is my mother, Lucy, and my dad, Freeman. I believe I've told you what they do for a living."

"A teacher and a mechanic, right?" Reo asked, reaching out to shake each parent's hand. Lucy looked him over thoroughly, and she wasn't the only one. Reo felt the heavy stares of her two giant-size brothers—that had to be them since they were the only twins he saw—and a strawberry blonde who looked so much like Rusty she had to be big sis.

Resisting the urge to run back around the house the way they'd just walked, Reo, instead, let Rusty introduce every relative who'd come together today to celebrate her brothers' birthdays. He met her siblings—he'd guessed correctly—her namesake aunt, assorted nieces, nephews and cousins, two uncles and a grandmother— enough relatives to shock an only child out of ten years' growth.

But I'm not an only child, Reo suddenly remembered, a thought that gave him courage to go on. Family was something he was going to have to get used to, it seemed.

"Dad's cooking his specialty," Rusty said, pointing to a huge pot, simmering on a portable cooking rig. "Shrimp gumbo."

"Ever eat it?" asked Bit, who still had a glint of suspicion in his eye.

"Many times," Reo answered. "It's a favorite of mine."

"Then you'll love Dad's," Rusty said, slipping her arm through Reo's and giving her brother a so-there look.

Reo liked the fact that she felt so protective. He could only hope he wouldn't need her to actually do battle for him.

"Dinner won't be ready for a while yet," said Spin. "Why don't we choose up sides and play volleyball?"

Rusty tensed. "I don't know if Reo—"

"Actually, that sounds like fun," Reo interjected. If nothing, he was physically fit. He would prove to these guys he was no wuss, thus winning their approval for him to...what? Have sex with their big sister? Something told Reo that would never go over big with this closely knit family. And that realization gave him new understanding of Rusty, not to mention her dreams and goals.

The game proved every bit as challenging as Rusty had warned. Bit could spike the hell out of the volleyball and did so more than once, but Reo, used to playing rough at the health club, held his own. In the end his stamina earned him the grudging respect of his teammates and the guys on the other side of the net.

It also earned him two scraped knees, a jammed finger and a wrist injury that necessitated a trip to the emergency room, much to Reo's embarrassment. To make matters worse, all Rusty's siblings, as well as Rusty herself, insisted on accompanying him there via Spin's minivan.

Fortunately the wrist was sprained and not fractured as everyone had feared. His arm in a splint and a sling, Reo made his way to the pay window just a half hour after his arrival at the hospital. He was asked to sit and did, waiting patiently while a receptionist took insurance information and tallied his bill.

Right beyond a portable partition, and clearly unaware of his proximity, sat Rusty and crew. On hearing his name, Reo tuned in to their conversation and was treated to a stinging dissertation by sister Mouse on the evils of the rich.

"I can tell you're in love with him."

"I am not," Rusty retorted. Reo heard the tremor in her voice and had to wonder how long she'd been in Mouse's line of fire.

"Yes, you are, and you'll be sorry if you don't break it off right now."

"Look, Mouse," Rusty argued. "Just because the rich man you married turned out to be a jerk doesn't mean all guys with money are."

"He seems nice enough to me," said one of the twins. Reo guessed it was Bit.

"Yeah," added the other brother. "I like him."

Thank the Lord for small favors. Reo took back his insurance card, which the receptionist had just copied, and stood, more than ready to get out of there.

"You won't think he's so cool when he breaks Rusty's heart," Mouse retorted just as Reo stepped back into the waiting area. Her eyes widened with shock, while Rusty's face blushed crimson.

Though tempted to set Mouse straight then and there, Reo didn't. Common sense said her not-so-little brothers would defend her. He wanted to keep them on his side.

"It's just a sprain," he therefore said, holding out his splinted arm.

"I'm so glad," Rusty gushed, leaping up to stand by him. She slipped her hand through his uninjured arm and leaned close. Her smile thanked Reo for ignoring Mouse and keeping the peace. Mad enough to chomp nails, he couldn't even fake an answering grin.

The men kept the conversation light on the drive back to the house and all during the setting up of the card tables at which they eventually sat. Reo, his spirits now lodged in his shoestrings, tried his best to get back into the swing of things and enjoy the spicy gumbo served by Rusty's jovial dad. It wasn't easy.

Did everyone here secretly agree with Mouse? he mused, glancing beyond his tablemates, Rusty, Bit and Bit's three-year-old son, BB. He decided they probably did and, seriously outnumbered, wondered how he'd ever be able to neutralize all the garbage these well-meaning relatives fed Rusty when he was out of sight.

After they finished eating, everyone participated in cleanup. Reo, who'd managed to eat his fair share of gumbo, wholly agreed when one of Rusty's uncles suggested a thirty-minute digestion break before the traditional cake and ice cream. Everyone else seemed to go for the idea, too, and dispersed to cluster into groups of laughing, talking relatives.

Reo, himself, sat alone at his table, having excused Bit and son to go to the bathroom and Rusty to see if she could help clean the kitchen. Looking around at all her kin, he felt decidedly overwhelmed, but still thought wistfully of participating in a family gathering of his own.

"Does it hurt?"

Reo jumped at the sound of the question, which came from Mouse's daughter, a pint-size bundle of energy with copper hair and eyes so dark he couldn't see the pupils. The child, whose name he couldn't recall, had come up from nowhere and now eyed his splint, wrapped with a bright blue Ace bandage.

"Not much," Reo told her, charmed. Except for the eyes, she could be baby Macy several years down the road. He guessed Rusty had probably looked just like this when a little girl, too.

"Will you read to me?" From behind her, she pulled out a Golden Book entitled, of all things, *The Saggy Baggy Elephant*. Reo eyed the book with some alarm. This book and another would make two he'd read aloud in the past thirty-something years.

"He doesn't have time to read to you, honey," said Mouse, who'd scurried up and now reached for her daughter's hand as though Reo were some ogre about to have her for dessert instead of birthday cake.

"Actually, I do," Reo interjected, taking the book and giving Mouse a hard look. The child, who appeared to be about four or five years old, climbed up into his lap.

Propping the book on the table in front of him, he began to read what proved to be an entertaining tale of an elephant inordinately worried about the fit of his skin.

When Reo finished the last page, he looked up to find he was now surrounded by every Hanson relative under junior high school age—six of them in all—plus a Brittany spaniel and a Boston terrier.

"Wead!" ordered BB, handing Reo yet another Golden Book. A quick glance around revealed that every child had just such a book. His jaw dropped.

"Party favors," a very familiar voice explained. Turning, Reo found Rusty standing right in back of him. She smiled, hugged him from behind and placed a kiss on the top of his head. Bending down, she then put her lips to his ear to whisper, "If kids and dogs like you, then you can't be all bad."

Reo had to laugh, and his laughter lifted his spirits as much as her sweet vote of confidence. He then read each and every book, much to the delight of the children and maybe their parents. At any rate, everyone seemed friendlier after that, including Mouse, who took pains to offer him a corner slice of birthday cake and a smile decidedly sheepish.

The party started to break up around eight that night. Reo, whose wrist ached, began to search high and low for Rusty soon after, but she was nowhere to be found. After several wild-goose chases, he followed Bit's advice to check the pond in the nearby woods and there found Rusty, skipping stones across the slate gray water.

"Did you see that?" she exclaimed when he walked up. "It bounced four times!"

"Bet I can beat you," he said, bending down to select the perfect missile. Thankful he'd sprained his left wrist and not his right, Reo then flipped his stone over the water. It bounced once, twice, three times, then sank like the rock it was.

Rusty bubbled with laughter. "So you can beat me, huh?"

"Guess I'm out of practice."

"You've done this a lot, then?"

"Enough. My mother's father had a lily pond."

"Ah." Taking his hand in hers, Rusty led the way to a nearby fallen tree. She sat and tugged on Reo's arm, indicating he should do the same.

By now it was dusky dark, thanks to the shadows cast by the tall trees blocking the western sky. The sound of croaking pond frogs filled the air. Some nearby crickets chirped harmony. Rusty heaved a gigantic sigh and rested her head on Reo's shoulder.

"I've been meaning to ask you all day if you've heard anything from Edward Stiles," Rusty said.

"Not yet, I'm sorry to say."

She raised her head and twisted around to look him in the eye. "You're disappointed?"

"Sure I am," Reo told her. Amazingly it was true. Now that he'd finally accepted the fact that he had a brother and sister, he really wanted to get to know them.

Rusty flashed him an approving smile and cuddled up again. "I hope today hasn't been too much of an ordeal for you."

"Besides that one little setback, I really had a good time."

"Mouse shouldn't have said those things. She's basing her opinion on one worthless jerk."

"Actually, I was referring to this," he said, raising the splint.

"Oh." She sighed again.

"I like your parents," Reo ventured, searching for the

words to properly explain all the lessons learned that day. "I can see why you believe in marriage. Hell, there have been times today that I believed in it myself." He got to his feet and pulled Rusty to hers, then engulfed her in a hug. "I was wrong about being three-fourths in love with you, babe. I'm really head over heels."

Rusty caught her breath. "You swear?" she asked, tipping her head back to look him in the eye yet again.

"I swear," Reo answered from the heart.

"I'm so glad," she murmured, burying her face in his shirtfront, clinging to him as if she never intended to let go. Reo barely heard her next words—the most precious words of all. "I love you, too."

"Then will you give us a chance?" he entreated. "I can honestly say I want you in my life forever."

There they were, the words Rusty had hoped for, prayed for, almost from the day she'd met him: words of love and the promise of a future together.

That meant marriage to her. Clearly, this day with the Hanson family had accomplished what she'd hoped it would and taught him the value of relationships. All that she lacked now was the "Will you marry me?" that would make a dream she'd harbored since childhood come true.

"Will you move in with me now, tonight?" Reo asked.

"Excuse me?"

"Will you share my house and my life? Oh, I know you want a wedding. I understand that, and while I'm not quite ready to walk down the aisle just yet, I swear I'm closer than I've ever been. I just need a little more time to get used to the idea."

"Time?" Flabbergasted, Rusty twisted free of his embrace and took a step back. "And just how much time are we talking here, Reo? A week, a month, a year, the rest of our lives?''

''How would I know?'' he answered, clearly baffled by her ire.

''So you have no idea how long it's going to take for you to make up your mind about me, yet you expect me to put my dreams and plans on hold indefinitely—''

Reo glanced around as if he thought their quarrel might be overheard. ''Could you just cool it, Rusty? I don't want to fight with you here, or anywhere else, for that matter.''

''Cool? You want cool? Then never, ever mention an affair to me again because that word *burns me up!*''

Dead silence followed her heated outburst. Reo pivoted sharply and walked to the edge of the pond, where he stood for long moments taking deep breaths and staring out over water now inky black. Rusty, sick of trying to reason with him, sat down on the log again.

Clearly they were still miles apart in their thinking and from all indications always would be. Love and commitment to him meant something else besides marriage and babies—just what, Rusty couldn't begin to imagine.

''I think it would be better if we just break this off right here and now,'' she finally said, letting her exasperation and temper get the best of her better judgment. ''It's obvious we're never going to want the same thing.''

''Fine,'' Reo snapped, spinning around to walk back to the log. His eyes glinted coldly in the dark.

''And I'd appreciate it if we could at least act friendly until we get away from here. I'm not up to an I-told-you-so call from my hotheaded sister tonight.''

Reo nodded his cooperation, probably because he

didn't want an encounter with Mouse, either. Fighting tears, Rusty led the way through the now-dark woods to the Hansons' house. She took Reo's hand in hers right before they exited the trees. It wasn't easy faking everyone out for the next ten minutes, but Rusty gave it her best shot, and so, to her relief, did Reo. No one could've guessed they weren't really the best of friends.

Once in the car and on their way home, however, neither said a word. When Rusty braked her car in Reo's drive sometime later, he got right out of the vehicle, strode quickly to his front porch and disappeared into his house without once looking back.

Rusty's eyes swam. So he could love and leave her that easily, huh? Giving in to the hot tears of disappointment spilling down her cheeks, she put the car in motion and headed for home. Two could play his game, she told herself as she pulled into her drive sometime later. The tears she'd cried tonight were tears too many.

It was time to forget Reo, a man she'd known better than to love right from the start. He had his money and all it would buy to keep him company. He'd never really need a flesh-and-blood woman with nothing to give him but moth-eaten dreams.

"Maybe you should take some time off," suggested Angie, who'd just taken dictation from Reo. Though it was only Wednesday, she'd suggested that same thing at least a dozen times that week.

"A vacation is the last thing I need," Reo growled at her, the next instant penitent. He'd been a bear since the fight with Rusty on Sunday. It was a wonder his secretary hadn't long since decked him. "I've got something on my mind, OK? A personal situation I have to work out somehow."

"Is Rusty Hanson involved?"

Reo tensed. "Why do you ask that?"

"I know the two of you went out, and since you haven't called her this week, I thought maybe you'd had a fight or something."

"You don't know every call I make, Angie. I can dial the phone myself."

"Since when?" she asked, a damn good question. As a rule, Reo hated the phone, so made Angie place all his calls.

"Would you please just get out of here?" he asked, glaring at her.

"I'm only trying to help." Without batting an eye, she gathered up her pencil and pad and obediently exited the room. Angie, who'd worked for him for years, was skilled in handling his mood swings and didn't take any guff—a damn good thing today.

Left alone in his office, Reo once again tried to figure out how in the hell he was going to live without Rusty, who now haunted his days and his nights. He wished he'd never revealed his desire for her. He'd known better. Hadn't every other woman in whom he'd ever shown the least bit of interest immediately expected a wedding? Just look at Colleen O'Shaunessy, for crying out loud. Why, they hadn't had three dates before she started buying *Bride* magazine.

Reo shivered at the chilling memory.

The difference between Rusty and Colleen, of course, was motive. And that, more than anything, drove him nuts. While Colleen wanted to marry him for his money and position, Rusty wanted to marry him in spite of it. How ironic, he realized, sitting back and letting his thoughts wander where they would.

Naturally they settled right on Rusty, a woman dif-

ferent from most, a woman who was all he'd ever need.
They were a match made in heaven for sure. So why
couldn't he give her what she wanted? What held him
back?

Could it be his barely acknowledged belief that if she
really loved him she'd understand and accept his terms?
Pleased to have found a possible reason for his resistance
to her game plan, Reo quickly decided that must be the
problem.

A businessman who was used to give and take, he
favored compromise when a solution appeared to be impossible. And was Rusty willing to compromise? No sir-
ree. She wanted everything her way. No wedding? No
relationship of any kind. *Finis*.

But just what compromise was there in this situation,
anyway? Reo gave the matter a good ten minutes'
thought before finally admitting there might not be
one—a truth that disturbed him. It seemed it came to
this, if he and Rusty were to have any kind of life together: either he got his way or she got hers.

If he got his way, then Rusty would be forced to give
up—at least for a time—a dream she'd apparently had
from a very young age. Reo could easily imagine her
playing with four baby dolls as a kid, pretending to be
their mommy. So was giving Rusty her dream worth the
sacrifice of giving up his own?

And did he even have a dream, anyway?

Chapter Ten

Reo frowned, trying to think of what he wanted most in the world. All he could think of was Rusty. He had everything else or could get it. *Then why am I holding back?* he asked himself yet again. The answer came to Reo at once—an answer so simple he marveled that he hadn't thought of it before: fear.

Simple fear.

But it wasn't her elopement idea that scared him. That actually sounded great, or he could handle tuxedos, preachers, and even judgmental in-laws, if Rusty changed her mind. It wasn't the four babies she wanted, either. He was finding that he liked kids, and now that he'd finally gotten used to the idea of having a family, actually figured the more the merrier. Heaven knew there could be no better mommy than Rusty, who had just the personality necessary to make raising children fun.

No, it was another fear that kept him from proposing to her—fear that he really wasn't the man she thought he was, fear that he would never manage to be the husband she needed, fear that he'd fail her.

Though usually a man willing to gamble, Reo realized that this time he was not. How could he afford the risk, when Rusty was the one who'd lose the most if things didn't work out?

"Hi, Mom."

"Well, hello, honey," answered Lucy Hanson when her daughter called on Thursday. "How has your week been?"

"Lousy, actually. Reo and I had a fight…a big fight." Absently, Rusty petted Bandit, stretched out beside her on her bedspread. "We haven't talked since Sunday, four whole days, and I'm beginning to wonder if we'll ever talk again."

"The lament of a woman in love, obviously. I'd guessed that already. And does he love you?"

"He says so," Rusty answered. "Frankly, I'm not sure he knows what the word really means."

"So he's not the marrying kind."

"How on earth did you guess that?"

"Not only did I have four brothers and a dad, I married a man who gave me two male children. I know the gender, dear, and I can say with authority that no man really wants to give up his freedom. It goes against the macho grain."

"Reo says he needs time, says he thinks he'll eventually get used to the idea of walking down the aisle."

"It took your father five years to come around."

"I'm twenty-eight years old. I want four children. I don't have five years."

"Then I suggest a compromise."

"Believe me," Rusty said. "If I could think of one, I'd call Reo right this minute and suggest it."

"Hmm. Well, as I see it, Reo doesn't want to get married right now, but thinks he might later, while you're afraid that will be too late for you to have the children you want. Right?"

"Exactly right."

"Then the answer is obvious. You simply offer him a time-limited relationship. Six months. A year. Whatever you think you can live with. If he still doesn't want to get married at the end of that time, then you move on."

"Broken heart and all?"

"I never said this solution would be risk free."

Rusty sighed the truth of that. "Actually, your idea is the best so far, risks and all. I just don't know if Reo will go for it."

"Maybe you should call him and find out."

"Yeah," Rusty said, coming to a sudden decision. "Maybe I should."

After telling her mother goodbye, she pressed the hang-up button a couple of times to clear the line. But instead of hearing a dial tone, as expected, she heard the voice of a woman who sounded vaguely familiar.

"Hello? This is Martha Crain. Is someone there?"

"Why, hello, Martha," Rusty answered, realizing she must have intercepted an incoming call before the phone even rang. "This is Rusty. How are you?"

"Fine, fine...though I'm up to my neck in preparations for a surprise appreciation dinner for Reo Saturday night. He just donated the money to build a pediatric wing at the hospital, and I think it's high time he was recognized for all his good works. I know this is very short notice, but I'm calling to see if you'll come."

"I'm afraid that Reo and I are currently at outs. My being there might not be such a wonderful idea."

"Oh, my dear, I'm so sorry to hear that. I can't tell you how excited I was last Saturday night when I realized how much Reo cares for you. Why, I said to Leo, 'Rusty's the one,' and he agreed. Poor Reo had such an unstable childhood, you know. I always worried that he might never understand the value of family. I honestly thought you were just the woman to teach him."

"Believe me, there's nothing I'd like to do more."

"Then come to my party. That might be all it takes to get the two of you together again."

"If only it would," Rusty murmured thoughtfully, picturing a romantic reunion with Reo. "You know, I think I will come. Thank you for asking me, Martha." Obviously thrilled by her decision, Rusty's new friend gave her all the pertinent information about the gala.

So Saturday night found Rusty at the very same country club she and Jade had crashed mere weeks—or was it an eternity?—ago. She felt older and wiser, but her palms sweated just as they had that fateful night.

Having arrived a little late, Rusty peeked into the dimly lit banquet hall to get her bearings. She saw a raised platform on which was placed the speaker's table. Reo sat there, along with Martha Crain and some other people Rusty did not recognize. In the glow provided by the floor and overhead spotlights that illuminated the table, he looked every bit the respected businessman, if a bit flustered, due, no doubt, to the fact that he hadn't realized his friends were gathering to honor him.

Rusty took note of Reo's elegant black tux and glanced down at her own borrowed finery, a slim, floor-length gown of palest cream crepe. The beautiful garment, adorned with beads and pearls, sparkled even in the low light provided by the candles sitting on each of the many tables dotting the room. Wearing it gave Rusty much-needed confidence, though not enough to find herself a seat and join the party.

Content to stay hidden in the shadows for a while longer, Rusty instead stood just inside the door and watched the proceedings. She quickly realized Reo's friends honored him with a "roast." Their speeches, mostly humorous, brought to light generosity Reo would never mention and she'd never imagined.

Rusty learned that he'd not only donated enough money to build a pediatric wing, but in the past had sponsored an oncology unit, too. He'd also paid for a school library, renovations to a charitable nursing home, and the playground equipment at one of Shreveport's public parks. Clearly he believed in using his wealth for the public good. Clearly he cared.

Her eyes swam with emotion in a matter of seconds. By the time the last speaker had his say, Rusty constantly swiped at her tears of pride to keep them from spotting the dress. Her heart swelled with love. Her doubts faded to foolish fears.

Rusty suddenly remembered her first impression of Reo, a man she'd known only as mail room Brad. That impression, it seemed, was the right one after all. Reo Sampson *was* a nice, nice man—the kind of man a girl could rely on every day, the kind of man worth altering a dream for any day.

Was it too late to tell him that she understood his worth? Rusty wondered. A whole week had gone by since their fight, and he hadn't called even once. Did that mean he'd given up on her, that he'd found himself another woman—one who recognized what a catch he was, one who was willing to give herself to him with no preplanned agenda, no time constraints and no strings attached?

Just then Martha introduced Reo. With obvious reluctance and not a little embarrassment, he got to his feet and walked slowly to the microphone while his friends—and Rusty—applauded like crazy. She heard the emotion in his voice as he haltingly began to speak. Suddenly overcome with the need to get closer, she eased forward and slipped into the nearest empty chair. Other guests at that particular table, their attention on Reo, barely noticed her arrival.

Rusty hoped Reo wouldn't notice it at all.

"I don't really know what to say," Reo murmured, sticking his hands into his pockets and rocking back on his heels like some little boy making his first speech at school. His eyes scanned the crowd as he talked, however, making a connection with each person and proving that he'd definitely spoken in public before. Rusty tensed every time his gaze swept by, but he never so much as blinked, proof he hadn't seen her.

Or maybe he had, she thought in response to a sudden burst of insecurity. Maybe he had, but no longer cared. Nervous, fearful of rejection, Rusty found that theory easiest to believe and actually thought about escaping.

"First," Reo said, glancing over at his hostess, "I want to thank Martha Crain, here, for throwing this shindig and lying to get me to come." He feigned a threatening look. "I won't soon forget this night, Marty."

Martha, clearly not intimidated, smiled sweetly at him. Rusty heard the laughter all around, but, lost in her gloom, could only brush a stray tear from her face.

"Next I want to thank you men for coming. I hate these monkey suits as much as you, so I appreciate the sacrifice you made to be here."

More laughter followed that.

"And last, but never least," Reo continued, his voice steadier. "I want to thank all you women. I know that if it weren't for each of you, the men wouldn't be here at all."

Once more the crowd expressed amusement.

"These folks, here," Reo then said, indicating his friends at the speaker's table, "have said a lot of nice things about me, but I haven't done anything so very special."

He turned his attention outward again and began to scan the occupants of the vast room as before, one…by…one. Rusty glanced toward the exit.

"I've just tried to do what's right—"

If he hadn't seen her already, he surely would now. Rusty considered bolting out the door, but knew that would get his attention for sure.

"—and that means—"

Maybe she could hide under the table.

"—putting my money—"

But no. She'd only get tangled in the crisp linen cloth draped over it.

"—where my mouth—"

Reo's gaze suddenly nailed her to her chair. He tensed. Rusty did, too.

"—m-my mouth—"

He fell completely silent then, almost as if dazed, and Rusty knew for sure that he had not spotted her before now. What's he thinking? she wondered, even as her heart began to hammer in her chest. Reo gave her no clue, but continued to stare. In seconds, people began to turn and search for the focus of his concentration.

He doesn't love me anymore, Rusty abruptly decided when he didn't speak. She stood, turned on her ridiculously high heel and headed straight toward the exit as she wished she'd done earlier.

"No, Rusty! Wait—"

Halting, Rusty turned slowly to face the platform just in time to see Reo leap right over some decorative potted plants onto the floor. In a heartbeat he stood by her side, no easy feat considering the maze of tables in the room.

"There's something I have to say to you," he said, grabbing her arm. "Something I just realized. God, what an idiot I've been." He slapped the palm of his free hand against his forehead. "I mean, here I stand, talking about how I put my money where my mouth is, when I haven't really done it at all. At least not when it mattered most." He shook his head in disbelief. "I told you I loved you, and I meant it. But I never followed through, did I?"

"What?…" How could she follow what he said when her head spun and her heart beat like a tom-tom?

"Oh, babe," Reo murmured, pulling her into his embrace. "Can you forgive me?"

"Whatever for?" she asked, certain the precious man who held her so tightly could never do anything that required an apology.

"For not following through with commitment." His words brushed over her flushed cheek, soft as the whisper they were.

"But commitment's not necessary anymore," Rusty answered, abruptly returning to her senses. She tipped her head back so she could see his eyes. "I've been selfish, Reo…trying to force my dreams on you, when—"

His finger to her lips halted her apology. Rusty tugged it away.

"No. I have to tell you this. I do." She drew a shaky breath. "What I'm trying to say is that if you still want me to, I'll move in with you. No promises, no strings, no pressure.''

Reo smiled tenderly. "You don't ask much."

"That way I won't—" Belatedly, Rusty halted the candid answer.

But Reo wasn't fooled. "Be disappointed?" He closed his eyes and swallowed hard. "I appreciate the gesture, but there's no need for it. I won't disappoint you again. In fact…" He glanced all around, then began to move toward the front of the room again, taking Rusty—trying to resist and not get tangled in her dress at same time—along with him.

"What are you doing?" she demanded in a panic of embarrassment.

Reo ignored her.

"Les?" he said when they reached the plants decorating the wooden platform.

Les Carson, one of the guests who'd roasted Reo earlier and now sat at the speaker's table, leaped to his feet and walked over to them. Turning, Reo caught Rusty by the waist and lifted her, struggling to hold the slit in her skirt together, into Les's waiting arms. He then accepted an assist to leap up beside them.

Laying an arm around Rusty's waist, Reo led her to the microphone. Rather than face the crowd—the talking, laughing, *very interested* crowd—Rusty closed her eyes and pretended she was a million miles away.

"You're all my friends or you wouldn't be here," Reo said to the audience. "And since you are, I want you to be part of the most important moment of my life so far." Covering the mike with his hand, Reo turned to Rusty and lowered his voice. "Open your eyes, Rusty."

She did with reluctance.

"Now I'm going to ask you a question. If you don't

want to humiliate me in front of all these dear people, you must say 'yes.' Understand?'' Though his eyes twinkled, Rusty sensed an underlying uncertainty she knew had nothing to do with fear of humiliation.

Hoping, praying she could guess the question, Rusty replied, ''Oh, I understand, all right, but I'm not promising anything until I hear the question.''

Reo groaned softly, but a smile now teased the corner of his mouth. With a glance at the crowd he removed the microphone from its stand, then abruptly dropped to one knee—an action that produced a collective gasp of surprise, a buzz of anticipation and scattered applause.

Reo took Rusty's hand in his free one. ''Beatrice Rusty Hanson, will you marry me?''

''Yes!'' Rusty immediately answered even before Reo could hand her the mike. But everyone in the room heard, anyway. Their cheers and applause proved that. And now, locked in Reo's warm embrace, Rusty reveled in the sound.

Epilogue

As the familiar strains of Wagner's "Bridal Chorus" filled the air, Reo's heart began to pound. His gaze ever on the back of the room, he waited for his bride-to-be to step into view, and when she finally did, had to swallow back the emotion that threatened his composure.

She looked even more beautiful than she had the first time he'd seen her, dressed in white and running to catch an elevator. She wore white again today, he realized, but this gown, which shimmered in the glow of candlelight, wasn't just a costume, worn in fun. It was a tangible expression of her love for him, a symbol of her commitment.

Reo remembered asking if she was an angel the first time they'd met. She'd laughed and told him no, but she was wrong. Proof was the miracles she'd worked on him, on his life, and there were more miracles to come.

"Friends, we are gathered together..."

"Glad you came today, Ed," said Reo as he shook the hand of Edward Logan Stiles, who, during the past, very hectic month, had become as good a friend as he was a lawyer.

"Wouldn't have missed this wedding for the world," replied Ed. Though they talked to each other, both their gazes were glued to the costar of today's nuptials, Rusty, who stood across the crowded reception hall, laughing with her sister—now Reo's sister-in-law.

In her bridal regalia, Rusty personified every groom's fantasy, and Reo felt a rush of pride. His fantasy had become reality—the biggest miracle of all—which meant his lonely nights were over.

"By the way," Ed said. "I have some news about your brother and sister, but since this is hardly the place to discuss it, why don't you call me when you and Rusty get back from your honeymoon."

Reo shifted his gaze from his beautiful wife to look Ed straight in the eye. "Can you give me the gist now?"

Ed smiled at Reo's show of impatience. "If you like. Thanks to the work of a private detective named Cord McEnroe who interviewed Linette Ashe's friends and read as many letters and legal records as he could find—"

"Linette Ashe is dead?" Reo interjected.

Ed nodded. "I'm afraid so. She died twenty-one years ago of pneumonia. From what Cord could gather, she fought alcoholism and drug addiction most of her adult years. I suspect that's what your grandfather's monetary settlement went to buy. At any rate, her health deteriorated rapidly until her death at fifty."

Reo sighed. He'd feared as much. "And her children?"

"Linette gave up her son for adoption at birth. She

kept her daughter, however, raising her in New Orleans. Mariah Ashe was fourteen when her mother died.''

"Who took care of her then?" Reo could not keep the distress out of his voice. It hurt to know what his sister, now a young woman, had been through...and so senselessly.

"The state. According to Cord, she graduated from high school, then went to beauty school. After she graduated from there, she began to work in a shop in New Orleans."

"She's there now?"

"No, and Cord hasn't been able to locate her elsewhere just yet. He did manage to get his hands on a photo, however."

"Do you have it with you?"

Ed looked a little surprised by the question, but nodded. "In my briefcase out in the car." He frowned and glanced around at the wedding guests now filling the room to capacity. "Are you sure you want to see it *now?* We could wait until—"

"Now, please."

Ed headed to the door at once. For the moment alone, Reo looked across the room at his bride and found her looking back. She tensed as though reading his need and a heartbeat later joined him, slipping her hand in his. "What's up?"

"Ed has a photo of my sister. He's gone to get it."

At once Rusty raised Reo's hand to her lips and kissed the back of it—understanding that sent a shiver down Reo's spine. Not for the first time he sent up a prayer of thanks for this precious woman so perfect for him.

When Ed returned a few seconds later, he gave Rusty a smile of apology, then handed Reo one of two photos he held. "Mariah."

Studying the wallet-size image, Reo saw an attractive brunette with stylishly cut hair and wide blue eyes.

"Why, she looks like you!" Rusty exclaimed, taking the photo. "Look at her eyes and the shape of her nose and even her mouth."

"You think?" Reo asked, frowning doubtfully.

"Oh, I do." Rusty glanced up at Ed. "Don't you?"

The lawyer nodded. "I noticed it at once, and just wait until you see the photo of your brother, Gabriel Dillard." He handed them another color photograph— this one a snapshot of a man standing by a huge pickup truck. Since he wasn't looking at the camera, Reo guessed the shot had been taken from a distance. Gabriel Dillard appeared to be the rugged type, judging from the clothing he wore. He, too, had dark hair, and even Reo saw the family resemblance this time.

"Oh, my," Rusty murmured. "The similarities in build and looks are really startling."

"Yes," Reo agreed, adding, "Tell me his story."

Ed hesitated, once more glancing around the room.

"It's okay," Rusty told him.

Ed nodded. "As I mentioned, Gabe, as he's called, was given up at birth. The man who adopted him was career military and died in Vietnam when the boy was ten. His mother remarried shortly afterward to a man Gabe apparently did not like. At any rate, he left home at eighteen and began a career as a wilderness guide. That's what he's doing now."

"I take it you know where he is," Reo said.

"He's in Washington State."

"A better life, it seems, than Mariah," Reo said. "But they both could've used my father's money, not to mention his love."

"And you could've used their friendship," Rusty added.

"Yeah." Reo shook his head, experiencing a sharp pang of regret. "Maybe it's not too late."

"Of course it's not too late," Rusty answered, squeezing his hand.

"Then you want me to proceed with contacting them?" Ed asked.

"I've just been given something few men get," Reo answered. "The chance to right a wrong. Yes, I want you to contact my brother and sister. And the sooner the better."

"I'll get on it right away." Ed extended his right hand, and, after Reo shook it, exited the reception hall, leaving the bride and groom as alone as two people could be in a room filled with laughing, talking well-wishers.

"Sorry about that," Reo murmured. "Ed wanted to wait until after we got back, but—"

"Mr. Impatient couldn't?" Rusty teased, eyes twinkling. She stood close—so close that Reo couldn't resist pulling her even closer and pressing his lips to hers.

Rusty melted to him, all woman and so willing that his knees threatened to buckle. Reo could barely find strength to break the kiss, but break it he did, rather than do something that might embarrass them both.

Rusty sighed as she pulled away. "How long do we have to hang around here? I mean, we've toasted each other and everyone else, cut and eaten the cake, smiled until my teeth hurt and even paid the preacher. Can't we leave now?"

"How in the heck would I know, *Mrs.* Impatience?" Reo retorted, reaching out to smooth her veil, which he'd inadvertently rumpled. "This is my first—and last I might add—wedding."

"Well, whether it's proper to leave or not, we're gonna. I've got plans for you, and I'm thinking you might have some for me." She tilted her head slightly and gave him a smile so sexy that sweat popped out on his forehead.

"Well...do you?" she softly questioned.

"Baby, I *do*," Reo assured Rusty, taking her hand again and leading her straight to the nearest door.

*   *   *   *   *

Silhouette Romance is proud to present *Virgin Brides,* a brand-new monthly promotional series by some of the bestselling and most beloved authors in the romance genre.

In March '98, look for the very first *Virgin Brides* novel,

THE PRINCESS BRIDE by Diana Palmer.

Just turn the page for an exciting preview of Diana Palmer's thrilling new tale...

Chapter One

Tiffany saw him in the distance, riding the big black stallion. It was spring, and that meant roundup. It was not unusual to see the owner of the Lariat ranch in the saddle at dawn lending a hand to rope a stray calf or help work the branding. Kingman Marshall kept fit with ranch work, and despite the fact that he shared an office and a business partnership with Tiffany's father in land and cattle, his staff didn't see a lot of him.

This year, they were using helicopters to mass the far-flung cattle, and they had a corral set up on a wide, flat stretch of land where they could dip the cattle, check them, cut out the calves for branding and separate them from their mothers. It was physically demanding work, and no job for a tenderfoot. King wouldn't let Tiffany near it, but it wasn't a front row seat at the corral that she wanted. If she could just get his attention away from the milling cattle on the wide, rolling plain that led to the Guadalupe River, if he'd just look her way...

Tiffany stood up on a rickety lower rung of the gray

wood fence, avoiding the sticky barbed wire, and waved her Stetson at him. She was a picture of young elegance in her tan jodhpurs and sexy pink silk blouse and high black boots. She was a debutante. Her father, Harrison Blair, was King's business partner and friend, and if she chased King, her father encouraged her. It would be a marriage made in heaven. That is, if she could find some way to convince King of it. He was elusive and quite abrasively masculine. It might take more than a young lady of almost twenty-one with a sheltered, monied background to land him. But, then, Tiffany had confidence in herself; she was beautiful and intelligent.

Her long black hair hung to her waist in back, and she refused to have it cut. It suited her tall, slender figure and made an elegant frame for her soft, oval face and wide green eyes and creamy complexion. She had a sunny smile, and it never faded. Tiffany was always full of fire, burning with a love of life that her father often said had been reflected in her long-dead mother.

''King!'' she called, her voice clear, and it carried in the early-morning air.

He looked toward her. Even at that distance, she could see that cold expression in his pale blue eyes, on his lean, hard face with its finely chiseled features. He was a rich man. He worked hard, and he played hard. He had women, Tiffany knew so, but he was nothing if not discreet. He was a man's man, and he lived like one. There was no playful boy in that tall, fit body. He'd grown up years ago, the boyishness driven out of him by a rich, alcoholic father who demanded blind obedience from the only child of his shallow, runaway wife.

She watched him ride toward her, easy elegance in the saddle. He reined in at the fence, smiling down at her with faint arrogance.

"You're out early, tidbit," he remarked in a deep, velvety voice with just a hint of Texas drawl.

"I'm going to be twenty-one tomorrow," she said pertly. "I'm having a big bash to celebrate, and you have to come. Black tie, and don't you dare bring anyone. You're mine, for the whole evening. It's my birthday and on my birthday I want presents—and you're it. My big present."

His dark eyebrows lifted with amused indulgence. "You might have told me sooner that I was going to be a birthday present," he said. "I have to be in Omaha early Saturday."

"You have your own plane," she reminded him. "You can fly."

"I have to sleep sometimes," he murmured.

"I wouldn't touch that line with a ten-foot pole," she drawled, peeking at him behind her long lashes. "Will you come?"

He lit a cigarette, took a long draw and blew it out with slight impatience. "Little girls and their little whims," he mused. "All right, I'll whirl you around the floor and toast your coming-of-age, but I won't stay. I can't spare the time."

"You'll work yourself to death," she complained, and then became solemn. "You're only thirty-four and you look forty."

"Times are hard, honey," he mused, smiling at the intensity in that glowering young face. "We've had low prices and drought. It's all I can do to keep my financial head above water."

"You could take the occasional break," she advised. "And I don't mean a night on the town. You could get away from it all and just rest."

"They're full up at the Home," he murmured, grinning at her exasperated look. "Honey, I can't afford vacations, not with times so hard. What are you wearing for this coming-of-age party?" he asked to divert her.

"A dream of a dress. White silk, very low in front, with diamanté straps and a white gardenia in my hair." She laughed.

He pursed his lips. He might as well humor her. "That sounds dangerous," he said softly.

"It will be," she promised, teasing him with her eyes. "You might even notice that I've grown up."

He frowned a little. That flirting wasn't new, but it was disturbing lately. He found himself avoiding little Miss Blair, without really understanding why. His body stirred even as he looked at her, and he moved restlessly in the saddle. She was years too young for him, and a virgin to boot, according to her doting, sheltering father. All those years of obsessive parental protection had led to a very immature and unavailable girl. It wouldn't do to let her too close. Not that anyone ever got close to Kingman Marshall, not even his infrequent lovers. He had good reason to keep women at a distance. His upbringing had taught him too well that women were untrustworthy and treacherous.

"What time?" he asked on a resigned note.

"About seven?"

He paused thoughtfully for a minute. "Okay." He tilted his wide-brimmed hat over his eyes. "But only for an hour or so."

"Great!"

He didn't say goodbye. Of course, he never did. He wheeled the stallion and rode off, man and horse so damn arrogant that she felt like flinging something at his tall head. He was delicious, she thought, and her body felt hot all over just looking at him. On the ground he towered over her, lean and hard-muscled and sexy as all hell. She loved watching him.

With a long, unsteady sigh, she finally turned away and remounted her mare. She wondered sometimes why she bothered hero-worshiping such a man. One of these days he'd get married and she'd just die. God forbid that he'd marry anybody but her!

That was when the first shock of reality hit her squarely between the eyes. Why, she had to ask herself, would a man like that, a mature man with all the worldly advantages, want a young and inexperienced woman like herself at his side? The question worried her so badly that she almost lost control of her mount.

The truth of her situation was unpalatable and a little frightening. She'd never even considered a life without King. What if she had to?

She rode home slowly, a little depressed because she'd had to work so hard just to get King to agree to come to her party. And still haunting her was that unpleasant speculation about a future without King...

But she perked up when she thought of the evening ahead. King didn't come to the house often, only when her father wanted to talk business away from work, or occasionally for drinks with some of her father's acquaintances. To have him come to a party was new and stimulating. Especially if it ended the way she planned. She had her sights well and truly set on the big rancher. Now all she had to do was take aim!

* * * * *

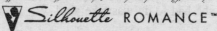

Take 4 bestselling love stories FREE

a FREE surprise gift!

Special Limited-time Offer

Mail to Silhouette Reader Service™

3010 Walden Avenue
P.O. Box 1867
Buffalo, N.Y. 14240-1867

YES! Please send me 4 free Silhouette Romance™ novels and my free surprise gift. Then send me 6 brand-new novels every month, which I will receive months before they appear in bookstores. Bill me at the low price of $2.90 each plus 25¢ delivery and applicable sales tax, if any.* That's the complete price and a savings of over 10% off the cover prices—quite a bargain! I understand that accepting the books and gift places me under no obligation ever to buy any books. I can always return a shipment and cancel at any time. Even if I never buy another book from Silhouette, the 4 free books and the surprise gift are mine to keep forever.

215 SEN CF2P

Name	(PLEASE PRINT)	
Address	Apt. No.	
City	State	Zip

This offer is limited to one order per household and not valid to present Silhouette Romance™ subscribers. *Terms and prices are subject to change without notice. Sales tax applicable in N.Y.

Return to the Towers!

In March
New York Times bestselling author

NORA ROBERTS

brings us to the Calhouns' fabulous
Maine coast mansion and reveals the
tragic secrets hidden there for generations.

For all his degrees, Professor Max Quartermain has a
lot to learn about love—and luscious Lilah Calhoun is
just the woman to teach him. Ex-cop Holt Bradford is
as prickly as a thornbush—until Suzanna Calhoun's
special touch makes love blossom in his heart.
And all of them are caught in the race to solve
the generations-old mystery of a priceless
lost necklace…and a timeless love.

Lilah and Suzanna
THE
Calhoun Women

**A special 2-in-1 edition containing
FOR THE LOVE OF LILAH and
SUZANNA'S SURRENDER**

Available at your favorite retail outlet.